Thomas Tindall Wildridge

The Grotesque in Church Art

Thomas Tindall Wildridge

The Grotesque in Church Art

ISBN/EAN: 9783337386900

Printed in Europe, USA, Canada, Australia, Japan

Cover: Foto ©Andreas Hilbeck / pixelio.de

More available books at **www.hansebooks.com**

The Grotesque . .

In Church Art . .

By T. Tindall Wildridge. . . .

LONDON :

WILLIAM ANDREWS & CO., 5, FARRINGDON AVENUE, E.C.

———

1899.

WILLIAM ANDREWS & C°

THE·HULL·PRESS

Preface.

THE designs of which this book treats have vast fields outside the English church works to which it has been thought good to limit it. Books and buildings undoubtedly mutually interchanged some forms of their ornaments, yet the temple was the earlier repository of man's ideas expressed in art, and the proper home of the religious symbolism which forms so large a proportion of my subject. In view also of the ground I have ventured to hint may be taken up as to the derivation, of a larger number than is generally supposed, of church designs from heathen prototypes by the hands of apprenticed masons, it is fitting that the evidences should be from their chisels. The only exceptions are a few wall-paintings, which serve to point a difference in style and origin.

In every case the examples are from churches in our own land. The conclusions do not nearly approach a complete study of the questions, the research to the present, great as it is, chiefly shewing how much has yet to be learned in order to accurately compare the extant with the long-forgotten.

The endeavour has been to present sufficient to enable general inferences to be drawn in the right direction.

Of the numerous works consulted in the course of this essay, the most useful has been "Choir Stalls and their Carvings," sketched by Miss Emma Phipson. While tendering my acknowledgments for much assistance obtained from that lady's book, I would add that the 'second series' suggested cannot but equal the first as a service to the cause of comparative mythology and folk-lore.

This place may be taken to dispose of two kinds of grotesques in church art which belong to my title, though not to my intention.

The memorial erections put into so many churches after the middle of the sixteenth century are to be placed in the same category as the less often ludicrous effigies of earlier times, and may be dismissed as "ugly monumental vanities, miscalled sculpture." The grotesqueness of some of these sepulchral excrescences may in future centuries be still more apparent, though to many even time cannot supply interest. Not all are like the imposing monument to a doctor in Southwark Cathedral, on which, by the way, the epitaph is mainly devoted to laudation of his *pills*. Yet, though the grotesque is not entirely wanting in even these monuments, it is chiefly through errors of taste. The worst of them are more pathetic than anything else. The grotesque proper implies a proportion of levity, whereas the earnestness evinced by these effigies are more in keeping with the solemnity of the church's purpose than the infinitely more artistic and unobtrusive ornament of the fabric. The other class of grotesque is the modern imitation of mediæval carving, with original design. Luckily, it is somewhat rare to find the spirit of the old sculptors animating a modern chisel. One of the best series of modern antiques of this kind is a set of gargoyles at St. Nicholas's, Abingdon, executed about 1881, of which I think it worth while to append a warning sample.

These two classes are left out of account in the following pages.

MODERN GARGOYLE, ABINGDON, 1881.

Contents.

A ROOF SUPPORTER, EWELME, OXON.

The Grotesque in Church Art.

Introduction.

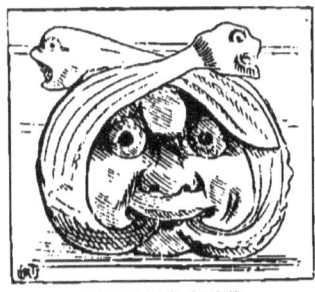

GORGONIC MASK, EWELME.

THE more lofty the earlier manifestations of man's intellect, the more complete and immediate seems to have been their advancement. That is to say, where the products of genius depend mainly upon the recognition of great principles and deliberate adherence to them, they are more satisfying than when success depends upon dexterous manipulation of material. What I have in view in this respect in connection with architecture has its co-relative in language. The subtlety and poetic force of Ayran roots shew a refined application of principle—that of imagery—in far advance of the languages rising from them. The successive growths of the detail of language, for use or ornament,—and the useful of one age would seem to become the ornamental of another—necessarily often forsake the high purity of the primeval

1

standard, and give rise, not only to the commonplace, but, by misconception or wantonness, to perversion of taste. So in architecture. Temples were noble before their ornaments. The grotesque is the slang of architecture. Nowhere so much as in Gothic architecture has the grotesque been fostered and developed, for, except for a blind adherence to ancient designs, due to something like gild continuity, the whole detail was introduced apropos of nothing. The assisting circumstance would appear to have been the indifference of the architects to the precise signi- ficance of the detail ornaments of their buildings. Gothic, or in fact any architecture admitting ornament, calls for crisp sub-regular projections, which shall, by their prominence and broken surface, attract the eye, but by the vagueness of their general form attract it so slightly as to lose individuality in a general view. These encrusting ornaments, by their opposition to the light of what the carvers call a "busy" surface, increase and accentuate rather than detract from the effect of the sweep of arches or dying vistas of recurring pillars. They afford a sort of punctuation, or measurers of the rhythm of the composition. Led from point to point, the eye gathers an impression of rich elaboration that does not interfere with its appreciation of the orderliness of the main design.

These objects gained, the architects did not, apparently, enquire what the lesser minds, who carved the boss or dripstone, considered appropriate ornament. Hence we have a thousand fancies, often beautifully worked out, but often utterly incongruous with the intent of the edifice they are intended to adorn, and unworthy of the architecture of which they are a part.

As in language the grotesque is sometimes produced by inadvertency and misconception, so in ornament not all the grotesque is of set purpose, and here the consideration of the less development of the less idea has its chief example. As original meaning became lost, the real merit of earnestness decreased, and the grotesque became an art.

Moreover, the execution of Gothic ornament is excellent in proportion to its artistic easiness. Thus the foliate and florate designs are better carved than the animal forms, and both better than the human. With the exception of little else besides the Angel Choir at Lincoln, and portions of the Percy Shrine at Beverley, there is nothing in Gothic representation of sentient form really worthy of the perfect conceptions of architecture afforded by scores of English churches. It may, of course, be considered that anything but conventional form is out of place as architectural ornament ; on the other hand, it must not be ignored that conventionality is a growth. It is only to be expected, therefore, that where the artist found character beyond his reach he fell readily into caricature, though it is a matter for surprise to find such a high standard of ability in that, and in the carved work generally. We find no instances of carving so low in absolute merit as are the best of the wall-paintings of the same periods.

The sources from which the artists obtained their

material are as wide as the air. A chief aim of this volume is to indicate those sources, and this is done in some cases rather minutely, though not in any exhaustively. The point of view from which the subject is surveyed is that the original detail of the temples entirely consisted of symbols of worship and attributes, founded chiefly upon astronomical phenomena: that owing to the gild organization of the masons, the same forms were mechanically perpetuated long after the worship of the heavenly bodies had given way to Christianity, often with the thinnest veil of Christian symbolism thrown over them. To this material, descended from remote antiquity, came gradually to be added a multitude of designs from nature and from fancy.

HARPY, EXETER.

RAGE AND TERROR, RIPON.

Definitions of the Grotesque.

THE term "Grotesque," which conveys to us an idea of humourous distortion or exaggeration, is simply *grotto-esque*, being literally the style of art found in the grottos or baths of the ancients. The term rose towards the end of the fifteenth century, when exhumation brought to light the fantastic decorations of the more private apartments of the licentious Romans. The use at that period of a similar style for not unsimilar purposes gave the word common currency, and it has spread to everything which, combined with wit or not, provokes a smile by a real or pretended violation of the laws of Nature and Beauty. In its later, and not in its original, meaning is the word applied to the extraordinary productions of church art. We may usefully inquire as to the causes of those remarkable characteristics of Gothic art which have caused the word Grotesque to fittingly describe so much of its detail.

The joke has a different meaning for every age. The capacity for simultaneously recognizing likeness and contrast between things the most incongruous and wide-sundered, which is at the root of our appreciation of wit, humour, or the grotesque, is a quality of slow growth among nations. No doubt early man enjoyed his laugh, but it was a different thing from the laughter of our day. Many races have left no suspicion of their ever having smiled; even where there are ample pictorial remains, humour is generally unrepresented. The Assyrians have left us the smallest possible grounds for crediting them with its possession. Instances have been adduced of Egyptian humour, but some are doubtful, and in any case the proportion of fun per acre of picture is infinitesimally small. The Greeks, perhaps, came the nearest to what we consider the comic, but with both Greek and Roman the humour has something of bitterness and sterility; even in what was professedly comic we cannot always see any real fun. Where it strikes out unexpectedly in brief flashes it is with a cold light that leaves no impression of warmth behind. The mechanical character of their languages, with a multitude of fixed formulæ, is perhaps an index to their mental development. The subtleties of wit ran in the direction of gratifying established tastes and prejudices by satirical references, but rarely condescending to amuse for mere humour's sake.

Where is found the nearest approach to merriness is in what now-a-days we regard as the least interesting and meritorious grade of humour, the formal parody. The Greeks had, outside their fun, let it be noted, something better than jococity, and that was joyousness. The later Romans became humourous in a low way which has had a permanent influence upon literature and art.

Sense of humour grew with the centuries, and by the time that the Gothic style of architecture arose, appreciation of the ludicrous-in-general (*i.e.* that which is without special reference to an established phase of thought) is traceable as a characteristic of, at least, the Teuton nations. It must be admitted that the popular verbal fun of the middle ages is not always easy to grasp, but it cannot be denied that where understood, or where its outlet is found in the graphic or glyphic arts, there is allied to the innocent coarseness and unscrupulousness, a richness of conceit, a wealth of humour, and a delicate and accurate sense of the laughable far beyond Greek wit or Roman jocularity.

It is to the embodiments of the spirit of humour as found in our mediæval churches that our present study is directed.

It may be as well to first say a little upon those comicalities which may be styled 'grotesques by misadventure.' This is a branch of the subject to be approached with some diffidence, for it is in many cases difficult to discriminate between that which was intended to be grotesque, and that which was

executed with serious or often devout feelings, but for one
of several causes often presenting to us an irresistibly comic
effect.

The causes may be five. First, the varying mechanical
and constructive incompetency of the artists to embody their
ideas. Second, the copying of an earlier work with executive
ability, with strong perception of its unintentional and latent
humour, but without respect to, or without knowledge of, its
serious meaning. Third, the use of symbolic representation,
in which the greater the skill, often the greater the
ludicrous effect. Fourth, the change of fashion, manners,
and customs. Fifth, a bias of mind which impelled to
whimsical treatment.

Consideration of the causes thus roughly analysed will
explain away a large proportion of the irreverence of the
irreverent paintings and carvings which excite such surprise,
and sometimes disgust, in the minds of many modern observers
of ecclesiological detail.

It will be seen that the placing of carvings in any one of
these five classes, or in the category of intentional grotesques,
must, in many cases, be a mere matter of opinion. For the
present purpose it will not be necessary to separate them,
except so far as the plan of the work does it automatically.
Many ecclesiastical and other seals afford familiar instances of
the 'comic without intention,' parallel to what is said above
as to carvings.

The Carvers.

LINCOLN. *14th cent.*

SEEMINGLY probability and evidence go hand in hand to shew that a great bulk of the church mason work of this country was the work of foreigners. Saxon churches were probably first built by Roman workmen, whose erections would teach sufficient to enable Saxons to afterward build for themselves. Imported talent, however, is likely to have been constantly employed. Edward the Confessor brought back with him from France new French designs for the rebuilding of Westminster Abbey, and doubtless he brought French masons also. Anglo-Norman is strongly Byzantine in character, and though the channels through which it passed may be various, there is little doubt that its origin was the great Empire of the East. Again, the great workshop of Europe, where Eastern ideas were gathered together and digested, and which supplied cathedrals and cathedral builders at command, was Flanders; and there is little doubt that during some five centuries after the Norman Conquest, Flemings were employed, in a greater or less degree, on English work. Italians were largely employed. The Angel Choir of Lincoln is one distinct witness to that. The workmen who

3

executed the finely-carved woodwork of St. George's Chapel, Windsor, King's College, Cambridge, and Westminster Abbey, in the sixteenth century, were chiefly Italians, under the superintendence of Torregiano, a Florentine artist. He was a fellow-pupil of Michael Angelo, and is best known by the dastardly blow he dealt him with a mallet, disfiguring him for life. The resentment of Lorenzo de Medici at this caused Torregiano to leave Florence. He came to England in 1503.

The architect, however, of King Henry VII.'s Chapel was Bishop Alcock, an Englishman, born at Hull, the already existing Grammar School of which place he endowed, and, perhaps, rebuilt. Many other architects of English buildings were Englishmen, probably the majority, and doubtless a large proportion of the workmen also,* but it would be idle to deny that imported art speaks loudly from work of all the styles.

The carved detail may be relied upon to tell us something, and it speaks of an original reliance upon the East, which was never outgrown. The carvings found in England are not marked by anything at all approaching a national spirit, even in the limited degree that was possible. Except for a few carvings of armorial designs, and still fewer with slight local reference, there are none in wood or stone which would not be equally in place in any Romance country in Europe. The carvings, also, in the Continental

---

* Early in the thirteenth century unruly converts of the Abbey of Meaux, Yorkshire, were, to humble their pride, made stonemasons, etc.

churches present familiar aspects to the student of English ornament.

But if we have yet to wait some fortunate discovery of rolls of workmen's names, with their rate of wages, we are not without such interesting information concerning the old carvers as is contained in portraits they have left of themselves. Just as authors sometimes recognize how satisfactory

AN INDUSTRIOUS CARVER, LYNN.

it is to have their "effigies" done at the fronts of their books, so have the carvers of old sometimes attached to their works portraits of themselves or their fellows, in their habits as they lived, in their attitudes as they laboured.

Our first carver hails from Lincolnshire. In 1852, when the Church of St. Nicholas, Lynn, was restored, the misericordes were taken out and not replaced, but passed as articles of commerce eventually to the Architectural Museum, Tufton Street, London. Among these is a view of a carver's studio, shewing the industrious master seated, tapping carefully away at a design upon the bench before him. There are three apprentices in the background working at benches; there are at the back some incised panels, and a piece of open screen-work. Perhaps we may suppose the weather to be cold, for the carver has on an exceedingly comfortable cloak or surcoat. At his feet reposes his dog.

There is an interesting peculiarity about these Lynn

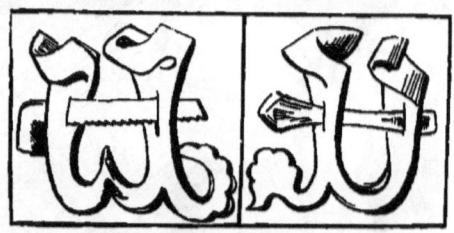

CARVER'S INITIALS, ST. NICHOLAS'S, LYNN.

carvings; the sides of the misericordes are designs in the fashion of monograms, or rebuses. The sides supporting the carver are his initials, pierced with his carving tools, a saw and a chisel. The difficulty is the same in all of the set; the meaning of the monograms is not to be lightly determined. In this case it may be U.V., or perhaps U is twice repeated.

The next carvers belong to the following century. Here also we see the principal figures in the midst of work. In this case, however, there has arrived an interruption. Either one of the workers is about to commit mock assault and battery upon another with a mallet, or a brilliant idea for a grotesque has just struck him, and he hastens to impart it. From the expression of the faces, and the attitudes for which two other workmen have stood as models, at the sides, the

COMMUNICATING A STRIKING IDEA, BEVERLEY MINSTER.

latter may be the more likely. It is not impossible that the carver of the fine set of sixty-eight misericordes in Beverley Minster had in mind the incident of the blow given to Michael Angelo, and it would be interesting to know if any of Torregiano's Italians worked at Beverley. This aproned, noisy, jocular crew are very different from the dignified artist we have just left, but doubtless they turned out good work of the humorous class.

The two "sidesmen" are occupied in the two ways of shewing intelligence and contempt known as "taking a sight," etc.

The next carver is a figure at Wellingborough, Northamptonshire. This is locally known as the Wellingborough shoemaker, but nearly all local designations of such things are wrong, and this is no exception. Elsewhere in speaking

MUTUAL CONTEMPT, BEVERLEY MINSTER.

of this sedate figure, I have conjectured he may be cutting something out of leather, and not making shoes. However, I have since arrived at Miss Phipson's conclusion : the figure can only be that of a carver. He is fashioning not a leather rosette, but a Tudor rose in oak, to be afterwards pinned with an oak pin in some spandrel. He is rather a reserved-looking individual, but a master of his craft, if we may suppose he has "turned out" the two eagles at his right and left.

No doubt there were several ways of building churches, or supplying them with their art decorations. Some masons would be attached to a cathedral, and be lent or sent here and there by arrangement. Others would be ever wandering, seeking church work. Others might come from abroad for particular work, and return with the harvest of English money when the work was done. For special objects there were depôts. It is an acknowledged fact that the black basalt fonts of Norman times were imported from

A PIECE OF FINE WORK, WELLINGBOROUGH.

Flanders. There are occasionally met other things of this material with the same class of design, evidently from the same source, such as the sculptured coffin-lid at Bridlington Priory, given on a following page. I have not seen it noted, but I think it will be established that "brasses," so much alike all over the country, were mostly ready-made articles also from Flanders. From the stereotyped conventionality of the altar-tomb effigies, they also may be judged to be the productions of workshops doing little but this work, and probably foreign.

What is required to determine the general facts on these points is a return from various fabric accounts. We shall probably find both English and foreign carvers. There is little or no doubt that the carvers of our grotesques were members of the mysterious society which has developed into the modern body of Freemasons. It would be interesting—if it were not so apparently impossible—to trace in the records of early Freemasonry, not only the names and nationalities of the masons and carvers, but the details of that fine organization which enabled them to develope ideas and improvements simultaneously throughout Europe; and which would tell us, moreover, something of the master minds which conceived and directed the changes of style. But the masonic history of our carvers is much enveloped in error to the outside world. Thus we are told that in the minority of Henry VI. the masons were suppressed by statute, but that on his assuming the control of affairs he repealed the Act, and himself became a mason; moreover, we are told he wrote out "Certayne Questyons with Awnsweres to the same concerning the Mystery of Maconrye" which was afterwards "copied by me Johan Leylande Antiquarius," at the command of Henry VIII.; the MS. being gravely stated to be in the Bodleian Library. No such MS. exists at the Bodleian Library. If it did, its diction and spelling (which is all on pretended record in certain books probably repudiated by the masonic body proper) would instantly condemn it as a forgery. Certainly an Act was passed, 3 Henry VI., which is in itself a historical monument to the importance of Freemasonry. It is a brief enactment that the yearly meetings of the masons, being contrary to the Statute of Labourers (of 25 Edward III., 1351) fixing the rates of labour, which the masons varied and apparently increased, were no longer to be held; offenders to be judged guilty of felony. The Commons did not quite know what to style the meetings, using in this short Act the following terms for them: Chapters, Assemblies, Congregations, and Confederacies.

But important though this proves the masons to have been, there is no account of the statute being repealed until the 5 Elizabeth, when another took its place equally intolerant to the spirit of Freemasonry, and Freemasonry really only became legal by the Act of 6 George IV.

But the prohibition of 1424 was not abolition. If the masons were debarred from being allowed to exercise their advanced notions of remuneration, or to have any legal recognition whatever, it scarcely seems to have affected their action. For if they had refrained from exercising their freedom, and submitted to being put down by statute, it is probable we should have met them in the form of more ordinary gilds as instituted by other craftsmen. But we do not meet them thus, and the inference is that they went on in their own way, at their own time, and at their own price. It may be presumed that the more or less migratory habits of the masons made the Act impossible to be rigidly enforced.

Coming down towards the end of Gothic times, we find, at any rate, there was one place where images might be

3

ordered.   In the Stanford churchwardens' accounts for 1556 there occur the following entries :—

"It.   In expences to Abyndon to speke for ymages   vijd.
It.   for iij ymages, the Rode, Mare, and John   xxijs. iiijd."

It will have been noticed that the portraits of the carvers are Late.   It is a great merit, on antiquarian grounds, that Gothic work, prior to the revival in art, was too much unconscious to admit anything so self-personal as a thought of the workers themselves, though frequently their 'marks' are unobtrusively set upon their works.   By the sixteenth century, the sculptor's art developed with the rest of mental effort, and the artists drank fresh draughts from the springs coming by way of Rome, springs whose waters had been concerned in the existence of nearly all the art that had been in Europe for ten centuries.

DOG AND BONE, BRECHIN.

The Artistic Quality of Church Grotesques.

THE grotesque has been pronounced a false taste, and not
desirable to be perpetuated. Reflection upon the causes
and meanings of Gothic grotesque will shew that perpetuation
is to be regretted for other than artistic reasons. If the taste
be false yet the work is valuable on historic grounds, for
what it teaches of its own time and much more for what it
hints of earlier periods of which there is meagre record
anywhere. Therefore it would be well not to confuse the
student of the future with our clever variations of imperfectly
understood ideas. Practically the grotesque and emblematic
period ended at the Reformation; and it was well.

But while leaving the falseness of the taste for grotesques
an open question, there is something to be said for them
without straining fact. For it is certain that there is underlying Gothic grotesque ornament a unique and, if not
understood, an uncopiable beauty, be the subject never so

ugly. The fascinating element appear to be, first, the completeness of the genius which was exercised upon it. It not only conveys the travestying idea, but also sufficiently conveys the original thought travestied.

What is it at which we laugh? It shall be a figure which is of a kind generally dignified, now with no dignity; generally to be respected, but now commanding no respect; capable of being feared, but now inspiring no fear; usually lovable, but now provoking no love. It shall be a figure of which the preconceived idea was either worthy or dreadful— which suddenly we have presented to us shorn of its superior attributes. Ideals are unconsciously enshrined in the mind, and when images proclaiming themselves the same ideals appear in sharp degraded contrast—we laugh. Thus we affirm the correctness of the original judgments both as to the great and the contemptible imitating it, for laughter is the effect of appreciation of incongruity. Custom overrides nearly all, and blunts contrast of ideas, yet wit, darting here and there among men, ever finds fresh contrasts and fresh laughter.

Further counts for something the excellence of the artistic management, which in the treatment of the most unpromising subjects filled the composition with beautiful lines. It was left to Hogarth's genius to insist on the reality of "the line of beauty" as governing all loveliness, and he suggests that a perceptive recognition of this existed on the part of the classic sculptors. This applies to their work in general, but he also mentions their frequent addition of some

curved object connected with the subject, as though it were a
kind of key to the artistic composition.   Whether consciously
or not, the ancients used many such adjunctive curved lines,
and Hogarth's conclusions cannot be styled fanciful.   The
helmet, plume, and serpent-edged ægis of Minerva, the
double-bowed bolt and serpents of Jupiter, the ornaments of
the trident, the aplustre and the twisted rope of Neptune, the
bow and serpent of Apollo, the plume of Mars, the caduceus
of Mercury, the ship-prow of Saturn, the gubernum or rudder

DOG AND BONE, CHRISTCHURCH, HAMPSHIRE.

of Venus, the drinking horn of Pan, together with many
another form to be observed in particular works of the
ancients, is each a definite and perfect example of the faultless
line.   Now, to repeat, many—an infinite number—of the
ornaments of Gothic architecture, and not less the grotesque
than any other description, are likewise composed of the most
beautiful lines conceivable, either entirely, or combined with
lines of abrupt and ungraceful turn that seem to deliberately
provoke one's artistic protest ; and yet the whole composition
shall, by its curious mixture of beauty and bizarre, its contrast

of elegance with awkwardness, leave a real and unique sense of pleasure in the mind. Doubtless the root of this pleasure is the gratification of the mind at having secretly detected itself responding to the call of art to exercise itself in appreciative discrimination. This may be unconsciously done; and in a great measure the qualities which give the

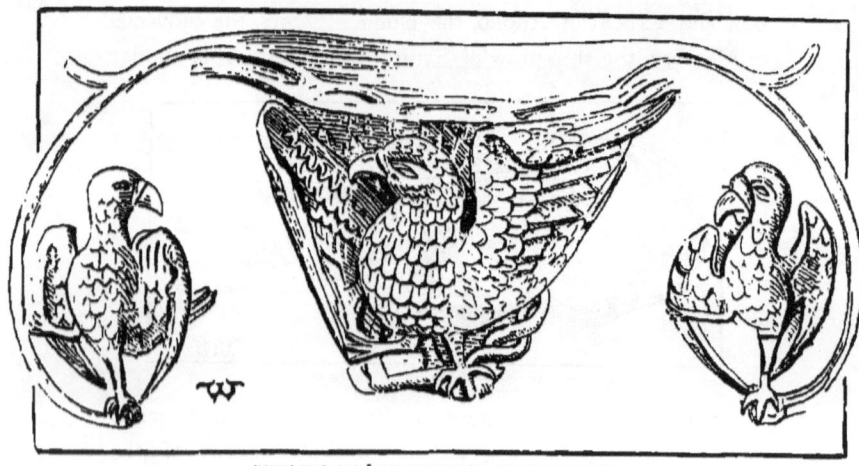

HAWKS OR EAGLES? WELLINGBOROUGH, NORTHAMPTONSHIRE.

pleasure would be bestowed upon the work in similar happy unconsciousness of the exact why and wherefore. Often, as in the ancient statues, a small curved form is introduced as an appendage to a mediæval grotesque.

Thus we see that there are combinations of two kinds of contrast which make Gothic grotesques agreeable, the artistic contrasts among the mere lines of the carvings, and the significatory contrasts evolved by the meanings of the carvings.

As far back as the twelfth century, a critic of church grotesques recognized their combination of contrasts. This was St. Bernard of Clairvaux, who, speaking of the ecclesiastical decoration of his time, paid the grotesques of church art the exact tribute they so often merit; probably the greater portion of what he saw has given place to succeeding carvings, though of precisely the same characteristics. He calls them "a wonderful sort of hideous beauty and beautiful deformity." He, moreover, put a question, many times since repeated by hundreds who never heard of him, asking the use of placing ridiculous monstrosities in the cloisters before the eyes of the brethren when occupied with their studies.

It is not possible to explain the "use" of perpetuating the barbarous symbols of a long-forgotten past; but it will be interesting to shew that there were actual causes accounting for their continued existence and their continued production, unknown ages after their own epoch.

Gothic Ornaments not Didactic.

R EFLECTION will not lead us to believe carvings to have been placed in churches with direct intent to teach or preach. Many writers have coincided in producing a general opinion that the churches, as containing these carvings, were practically the picture (or sculpture) galleries and illustrated papers for the illiterate of the past. This supposition will not bear examination. It would mean that in the days when humble men rarely travelled from home, and then mostly by compulsion, to fight for lord or king, or against him, the inhabitant of a village or town had for the (say) forty years sojourn in his spot of Merrie England, a small collection of composite animals, monsters, mermaids, impossible flowers, etc.—with perhaps one doubtful domestic scene of a lady breaking a vessel over the head of a gentleman who is inquisitive as to boots—with which to improve his mind. Sometimes his church would contain not half-a-dozen forms, and mostly not one he could understand or cared to interpret.

Misericordes, the secondary seats or shelves allowed as a relaxation during the ancient long standing services, are invariably carved, and episode is more likely to be found there than anywhere else in the church. Hence, misericordes have been specially selected for this erroneous consideration of ornament to be the story-book of the Middle Ages. This is unfortunate for the theory, for they were placed only in churches having connection with a monastic or collegiate establishment. They are in the chancels, where the feet of laymen rarely trod, and, moreover, there would be few hours out of the twenty-four when the stalls would not be occupied by the performers of the daily offices or celebrations.

The fact appears to be that the carvings were the outcome of causes far different from an intention to produce genre pictures. It is patent that anything which kept within its proper mechanical and architectural outline, was admitted. What was offered depended upon a multitude of considerations, but chiefly upon the traditions of mason-craft. The Rev. Charles Boutell has an apt description touching upon the origin of the carvings : calling them "chronicles," he says they were " written by men who were altogether unconscious of being chroniclers at all. . . . They worked under the impulse of motives altogether devoid of the historical element. They were influenced by the traditions of their art, by their own feelings, and were directed by their own know-ledge, experience, and observation, and also by the associations of their every-day lives." This appears to explain in general terms the sources of iconography. In brief, the sculptor had a stock-in-trade of designs, which he varied or supplemented, according to his ability and originality.

That the stock-in-trade, or traditions of the art, handed

4

down from master to apprentice, generation after generation, persistently retained an immense amount of intellectualia thus derived from a remote antiquity, is but an item of this subject, but the most important of which this work has cognizance.

SEA-HORSE DRAGONIZED, LINCOLN, *14th cent.*

Ingrained Paganism.

WE at this day may be excused for not participating in the good St. Bernard's dislike to the "hideous beauties" of the grotesque, and for not deploring, as he does, the money expended on their production. For many of them are the embodiments of ideas which the masons had perpetuated from a period centuries before his time, and which could in no other way have been handed down to us. There are many reasons why books were unlikely media for early times; for later, the serious import of the origin of the designs would be likely to be doubted; and for the most part the special function of the designs has been the adornment of edifices of religion. They were, in fact, religious symbols which in various ages of the world have been used with varying degrees of purity. One of the Rabbis, Maimonides, has an instructive passage on the rise of symbolic images. Speaking of men's first falling away from a presumed early pure religion he says :—"They began to build temples to the stars, . . . and this was the root of idolatry . . . and the false prophet showed them the image that he had feigned out of his own heart, and said it was the image of that star which was made known to him by prophecy; and they began after this manner to make images in temples and under trees . . . and this thing was spread throughout the world—to serve

images with services different one from another and to
sacrifice unto, and worship them. So in process of time the
glorious and fearful name was forgotten out of the mouth of
all living . . . and there was found on earth no people
that knew aught save images of wood and stone, and temples
of stone which they built." The ancient Hindoo fables also
indicate how imagery arose ; they speak of the god Ram," who,
having no shape, is described by a similitude." The worship
of the "Host of Heaven" was star-worship, or "Baalim."

The Sabean idolatry was the worship of the stars, to
which belongs much of the earlier image carving, for the
household gods of the ancient Hebrews, the Teraphim (as
the images of Laban stolen by Rachel), were probably in
the human form as representing planets, even in varying
astronomical aspects of the same planet. They are said to
have been of metal. The ancient Germans had similar
household gods of wood, carved out of the root of the
mandragora plant, or alraun as they called it, from the
superstition kindred to that of the East, that the images
would answer questions (from *raunen* to whisper in the ear).
Examination of many ancient Attic figurines appears to shew
that they had a not unsimilar origin, reminding us that both
Herodotus and Plato state the original religion of the Greeks
to have been star-worship, and hence is derived the Θεὸς
god, from Θεῖν to run. Thus in other than the poet's
sense are the stars "elder scripture."

A large number of the forms met in architectural
ornament, it may be fittingly reiterated, have a more or less

close connection with the worships which existed in times long
prior to Christianity. A portion of them was continuously
used simply because the masons were accustomed to them, or
in later Gothic on account of the universal practice of copying
existing works ; unless we can take it for granted in place of
that practice, that there existed down to Reformation days
"portfolios" of carver's designs which were to the last handed
down from master to apprentice, as must have undoubtedly
been the case in earlier times.   Other portions of the ancient
worship designs are found in Christian art because they were
received and grafted upon the symbolic system of the Church's
teaching.   The retention of these fragments of superseded
paganism does not always appear to have been of deliberate
or willing intention.   The early days of the Church even after
its firm establishment, were much occupied in combating
every form of paganism.   The converts were constantly
lapsing into their old beliefs, and the thunders of the early
ecclesiastical councils were as constantly being directed against
the ancient superstitions.   Sufficient remains on record to
shew how hard the gods died.

     To near the end of the fourth century the chief
intelligence of Rome publicly professed the Olympic faith.
With the next century, however, commenced a more
or less determined programme of persecutory repression.
Thus, councils held at Arles about 452 ruled that a
bishop was guilty of sacrilege who neglected to extirpate the
custom of adoring fountains, trees, and stones.   At that of
Orleans in 533 Catholics were to be excommunicated who

returned to the worship of idols or ate flesh offered to idols. At Tours in 567 several pagan superstitions were forbidden, and at Narborne in 590; freemen who transgressed were to have penance, but slaves to be beaten. At Nicea in 681 image worship was allowed of Christ.* At Augsburgh (?) in 742 the Count Gravio was associated with the Bishop to watch against popular lapses into paganism. In 743 Pepin held a council in which he ruled, as his father had done before, that he who practised any pagan rites be fined 15 sous ($\frac{15}{20}$ of a livre). To the orders was attached the renunciation, in German, of the worship of Odin by the Saxons, and a list of the pagan superstitions of the Germans. The Council of Frankfort in 794 ordered the sacred woods to be destroyed. Constantinople had apparently already not only become a channel for the conveyance of oriental paganism in astro-symbolic images, but was also evidently nearer to the lower idolatry of heathenism than the Church of the West. Thus we find the bishops of Gaul, Germany, and Italy in council at Frankfort, rejecting with anathema, and as idolatrous, the doctrines of the Council of Constantinople upon the worship of images.

While all this repression was going on, the Church was

* Of Christ, the Virgin, and saints only. It is here quoted as evidence of a tendency. It is plain that the council protected itself, for the following distich is attributed to it, which sums up the original intent of all images—

"Id Deus est, quod Imago docet, sed non deus ipse;
Hanc Videas, sed mente colas; quod cernis in ipse."

which Prideaux, Bishop of Worcester, translates (1681):

"A God the Image represents,
But is no God in kind;
That's the eye's object, what it shews
The object of the mind."

making itself acceptable, just as the Mosaic system had done in its day, by assimilating the symbols of the forbidden faiths. Itself instituted without formularies or ceremonial, both were needed when it became a step-ladder of ambition and the expedient displacer of the corrupt idolatries into which sun-worship had disintegrated. Hence among the means of organization, observance and symbol took the place of original simplicity, and it is small wonder that ideas were adopted which were already in men's minds. Elements of heathenism which, after the lapse of centuries, still clung to the Church's robes, became an interwoven part of her dearest symbolism. If men did not burn what they had adored, they in effect adored that which they had burned.

In spite, however, of edicts and adoptions, paganism has never been entirely rooted out; what Sismondi calls the "rights of long possession, the sacredness of time-hallowed opinion, and the potency of habit," are not yet entirely overcome in the midst of the most enlightened peoples. The carvings which point back to forgotten myths have their parallels in curious superstitions and odd customs which are not less venerable.

There were many compromises made on account of the ineradicable attachment of the people to religious customs into which they were born. Christian festivals were erected on the dates of heathen observances. In the sixth century, Pope Gregory sent word to Augustine, then in England, that the idolatrous temples of the English need not be destroyed, though the idols should, and that the cattle sacrificed to the heathen deities should be killed on the anniversary of dedication or on the nativities of the saints whose relics were within the church.

It is said that it was, later, usual to bring a fat buck into St. Paul's, London, with the hunters' horns blowing, in the midst of divine service, for the cathedral was built on or near the site of a former temple of Diana. This custom was made the condition of a feudal tenure. The story of Proserpine, another form of Diana, was the subject of heathen plays, and down to the sixteenth century the character appears in religious mystery plays as the recipient of much abuse.

Ancient mythology points in one chief direction. "Omnes Deos referri ad solem," says Macrobius, "All Gods refer to the sun," and in the light of that saying a thousand complicated fables of antiquity melt into simplicity. The ancient poets called the sun (at one time symbolically of a First Great Cause, at another absolutely) the Leader, the Moderator, the Depository of Light, the Ordainer of human things ; each of his virtues was styled a different god, and given its distinct name. The moon also, and the stars were made the symbols of deities. These symbols put before the people as vehicles for abstract ideas, were quickly adopted as gods, the symbolism being disregarded, and the end was practically the same as that narrated by the ancient rabbi just quoted. But it may be doubted whether the pantheism of the classic nations was ever entirely gross. The great festivals of the gods were accompanied by the initiation of carefully selected persons into certain mysteries of which no description is extant.

Thirlwall hazards the conjecture "that they were the remains of a worship which preceded the rise of the Hellenic mythology . . . grounded on a view of nature less fanciful, more earnest and better fitted to awaken both philosophical thought and religious feeling." Whether a purer system was unfolded to the initiated on these occasions or not, there is little doubt that it had existed and was at the root of the symbol rites.

AN IMP ON CUSHIONS, CHRISTCHURCH, HANTS., *early 16th cent.*

Mythic Origin of Church Carvings.

TAU CROSS,
WELLINGBOROUGH.

HE discoveries in Egypt in recent years un-doubtedly press upon us the fact that there was in Europe an early indigenous civilization, and that the exchange of ideas between East and West was at least equal. For the purpose of this study, however, the theory of independence is not accepted absolutely; it is premised that though there were in numerous parts of the old world early native systems of worship of much similarity, yet that such relics of them as are met in archi-tecture came from the East.

The mythic ideas at the root of Gothic decoration were probably early disseminated through Europe in vague and varying ways, whose chief impress is in folk-lore; but the con-crete forms themselves appear to have been introduced later, after being brought, as it were, to a focus, being selected and assimilated at some great mental centre. Alexandria was the place where Eastern and Western culture impinged on each other, and resulted in a conglomerate of ideas. These ideas, however, were not essentially different in their nature, though each school, Assyrian, Babylonian, Egyptian, Greek, and Hebrew, had diverged widely if they came from an un-known common source. But if Alexandria was the furnace in which the material was fused, Byzantium appears to have been the great workshop where the results were utilized, and from whence they were issued to Europe.

Sculptured ornament is not alone in the fact of its being a direct legacy from remotely ancient forms, though, on comparing that with any of the other arts hitherto recognized as of Eastern origin, it will be found that none bears such distinct marks of its parentage, or shews such continuity of form.   Thus examination of European glazed pottery, which comes perhaps the nearest to our subject, shews that the ornamenting devices occasionally betray an acquaintance with the old symbolic patterns, but there is less recognition of meaning, scarcely any intention to perpetuate idea, and no continuity of design.   It was not in the nature of the potter's purpose that there should be any of these, the difference being that for the mason's and the sculptor's art there was a very close association with the gild system.   The first Christian sculptors would be masons brought up in pagan gilds, and the gild instincts and traditions had undoubtedly as strong an effect upon their work, on the whole, as any religious beliefs they might possess.

The symbolism of the animals of the church in the late points of view of the Bestiaries and of the expository writers of the Middle Ages, is not here to be made the subject of special attention.   That is a department well treated in other works, particularly in the volume, "Animal Symbolism in Ecclesiastical Architecture," by Mr. E. P. Evans, which yet remains to be equalled.   It is to be noted, however, that the early

Christians, seeing the animals and their compounds so integral
a portion of pagan imagery, endeavoured to twist every
meaning to one sufficiently Christian : but what is chiefly
worthy of note is the unconscious resistance of the sculptors
to the treatment.   Although a multitude of figures can be
traced as used symbolically in accordance with the Christian
dicta, there are at least as many which shew stronger affinity
to pagan myth.   There is evidence that this was early recognized by the propogandists.   The Council of Nice in
787, in enjoining upon the faithful the due regard of images,
ordered that the works of art were not to be drawn from the
imagination of the painters, but to be only such as were
approved by the rules and traditions of the Catholic Church.
So also ordained the Council of Milan in 1565.

The Artists, however, did not invent the images so much
as use old material, and, the injunctions of the Council notwith-
standing, the ancient symbols apparently held their ground.
The protests of St. Nilus, in the fifth century, against animal
figures in the sanctuary, were echoed by the repudiations of
St. Bernard in the twelfth and Gautier de Coinsi in the
thirteenth, a final condemnation being made at the Council of
Milan in 1565, all equally in vain.   Though the force of the
myth symbols has passed away, they have left another legacy
than the grotesques of church art.   The art works of the
Greeks arose from the same materials, the glorious statues
and epics being the highest embodiment of the symbolic, so
loftily overtopping all other forms by the force of supreme
physical beauty as to almost justify and certainly purify the

religion of which they were the outcome ; so, later, the same ideas clothed with the moral beauty of supreme unselfishness enabled Christianity to take hold of the nations.

By the diatribes of Bernard we can see what materials were extant in the twelfth century for a study of worship-symbols and of the grotesque, though he ignores any possible meaning they may have.   He says, "Sometimes you may see many bodies under one head ; at other times, many heads to one body ; here is seen the tail of a serpent attached to the body of a quadruped ; there the head of a quadruped on the body of a fish.   In another place appears an animal, the fore half of which represents a horse, and the hinder portion a goat.   Elsewhere you have a horned animal with the hinder parts of a horse ; indeed there appears everywhere so multi-farious and so wonderful a variety of diverse forms that one is more apt to con over the sculptures than to study the scriptures, to occupy the whole day in wondering at these than in meditating upon God's law."

It has now to be observed how far the symbolic fancies of ancient beliefs have left their impress on the grotesque art of our churches.

A common representation of the great sun-myth was that of two eagles, or dragons, watching one at each side of an altar. These were the powers of darkness, one at each limit of the day, waiting to destroy the light.   This poetic idea has come down to us in many forms.   Greek art was unconsciously frequent in its use of the form, and mediæval sculptors, being often quite ignorant of the significance of the design, use it in a variety of ways, in many of which the likeness to the original is entirely lost, the composition ending in but a semi-

THE ALTAR OF LIGHT AND THE BIRDS OF DARKNESS, LINCOLN.

natural representation of birds pecking at fruit.   In the above block from Lincoln Minster, the altar is well preserved.   In the next block, which is from a carving connected with the preceding one, the idea is more distantly hinted at.

SYMBOLS OF DARKNESS, LINCOLN.

At Exeter, an ingenious grotesque composition of two duck-footed harpies, one on either side of a *fleur-de-lis*, is evidently from the same source.   Examples of this could be multiplied very readily.

THE ALTAR OF LIGHT AND THE BIRDS OF DARKNESS, EXETER.

The Cat and the Fiddle are subjects of carvings at Beverley and at Wells.

Man has an almost universal passion for the oral transmission of the fruits of his mental activity.   In the particular instances of many lingual compositions this passion has become an inveterate race habit, and the rhymes or reasons have been transmitted verbally to posterity long after their original meaning has been lost or obscured.   It is no new thing that a nursery rhyme has been found to be the relic of an archaic poem long misunderstood or perverted.   The lines as to " the cat and the fiddle " are an excellent instance of the

aptitude to continue the use of metrical composition the sense
of which has departed.   The full verse is, as it stands, a
curious jumble of disconnected sentences.

THE WEEKS DANCING TO THE MUSIC OF THE MONTH, BEVERLEY MINSTER

" Hey, diddle, diddle, the cat and the fiddle,
     The cow jumped over the moon,
The little dog laughed to see such sport,
     While the dish run away with the spoon."

HEY, DIDDLE, DIDDLE, THE CAT AND THE FIDDLE, WELLS.

I am not aware that any attempt has yet been made to
explain this extraordinary verse.   Examination seemingly
shews that it was originally a satire in derision of the worship
of Diana.   The moon-goddess had a three-fold existence.   On

the earth she was Diana.   Among the Egyptians we find her
as Isis, and her chief symbol was the cat.   Apuleius calls her
the mother of the gods.   In the worship of Isis was used a
musical instrument, the sistrum, which had four metal bars
loosely inserted in a frame so as to be shaken ; on the apex of
this frame, which was shaped not unlike a horse-shoe, was
carved the figure of a cat, as emblematic of the moon.   The
four bars are said by Plutarch to represent the elements, but
it is more likely they were certain notes of the diapason.
The worship of Isis passed to Italy, though the Greeks had
previously connected the cat with the moon.   The fiddle, as
an instrument played with a bow, was not known to classic
times, but the word for fiddle—*fides*—was applied to a lyre.
It is equivalent to a Greek word for gut-string.   In the light
of what follows, I suggest that " the Cat and the Fiddle " is a
mocking allusion to the worship of Diana upon earth.

In the heavens the moon-goddess had the name of Luna,
and her chief symbol was the crescent, which is sometimes
met figured as a pair of cow's horns.   Images of Isis
were crowned with crescent horns ; she was believed to
be personified in the cow, as Osiris was in the bull, and her
symbol, a crescent moon, is met in sculpture over the back of
the animal.   This apparently suggested the second line.

The third personality of the goddess was Hecate, which
was the name by which she was known in the infernal
regions,—which means of course, in nature, when she was
below the horizon.   Now another name by which she was
known was Prosperine (Roman), and Persephone (Greek),

and her carrying down into Hades by Pluto (Roman), or Dis (Greek), was the fable wrought out of the simple phenomenon of moon-set. I suggest that the last line of the verse is a grotesque rendering of the statement that—

"Dis ran away with Persephone."

Dis is equivalent to Serapis the Bull, otherwise Ammon, Æsculapius, Nilus, etc., that is, the Sun. Why the little dog laughed to see such sport is not easy to explain. It may be an allusion to one of the heads of Hecate, that of a dog, to indicate the watchfulness of the moon. There is another Hecate (a bad, as the above-mentioned was considered a beneficient diety), but which was originally no doubt the same, whose attributes were two black dogs, *i.e.*, the darkness preceding and following the moonlight in short lunar appearances. Or it may be an allusion to the fact that the dog was associated with Dis, being considered the impersonation of Sirius the Dog-star. In various representations of the rape of Prosperine, Dis is accompanied by a dog, *e.g.*, the grinning hound in Titian's picture.

Prosperine's symbol of a crescent moon was adopted as one of those of the Virgin Mary, and Candlemas Day, 2nd February, takes the place of the Roman festival, the candles used to illustrate the text, "a light to lighten the Gentiles," being the representatives of the torches carried in the processions which affected to search for the lost Prosperine.

Hindoo mythology has also a three-fold Isis, or moon-goddess; namely, Bhu on earth, Swar in heaven, Pátála, below the earth.

The moon-deity has not come down to us as in every case a female personation.   This is, however, explained by an early fable [in the Puránas] of the Hindoos, in which it is narrated that Chandra, or Lunus, lost his sex in the forest of Gauri, and became Chandri, or Luna.   The origin of this has yet to be discovered; it may be nothing more than the account of an etymological change, produced by a transcript of dialect.

Whether the Beverley artist knew that the cat was a moon-symbol may be doubted.   The fiddle has four strings, as the sistrum had four bars.   As well as the elements and the four seasons of the year, the four may mean the four weeks.   It will be observed that as the Hours are said to dance by the side of the chariot of the sun, so here four weeks dance to the music of the moon-sphere; the word moon means the measurer, and the cat is playing a dance measure!

The cat is not a very frequent subject.   At Sherborne she is shewn hanged by mice, one of the retributive pieces which point to a confidence in the existence of something called justice, not always self-evident in the olden-time. Rats and mice are the emblem of St. Gertrude.   The dog had a higher place in ancient estimation than his mention in literature would warrant; the fact that among the Romans he was the emblem of the Lares, the household gods, is a weighty testimonial to that effect, while the Egyptians had a city named after and devoted to the dog.

Among the pre-existing symbols seized by the Christians, the Egyptian Cross and Druidical Tau must not be overlooked.   It is found on the capitals of pillars at Canterbury and other places ; the example given in the initial on page 34 is perhaps the latest example in English Gothic.   Its admission as a grotesque is due to its, perhaps merely accidental, use as a mask as noted in the chapter on '' Masks and Faces.''

The sinuous course of the sun among the constellations is mentioned in literature as far back as Euripides as an explanation of the presence of the dragon in archaic systems of mythology.   This may have been the origin of the figure. Yet in addition to that there always seems to have been the recognition of an evil principle, of which by a change of meaning, the dragonic or serpentine star-path of the sun was made the personification or symbol.   According to Pausanius the '' dragon '' of the Greeks was only a large snake.

It might not be impossible to collect several hundreds of names by which the deistic character of the sun has been expressed by various peoples ; and the same applies, though in a less degree, to the Darkness, Storm, Cold, and Wet, which are taken as his antithesis.   One of the oldest of these Dragon-names is Typhon, which is met in Egyptian mythology.   Typhon is said to be the Chinese *Tai-fun*, the hot wind, and, if this be so, doubtless the adverse principle was taken to be the spirit of the desert which ever seeks to embrace Egypt in its arid arms.   The symbol of Typhon was the crocodile, and doubtless the dragon form thus largely rose.   Ráhu, an evil deity in Hindoo mythology, though generally called a dragon, is sometimes met represented as a crocodile, and his numerous progeny are styled crocodiles. The constellation called by the Japanese the crocodile is that known to us as the dragon.   Can it be that in the universal dragon we have a chronicle of our race's dim recollection of some survival of the terrible Jurassic reptiles, and hence of their period ?

But the myth has ever one ending ; the power of the evil one is destroyed for a time by the coming of the sun-god, though eventually the evil triumphs, that is dearth recurs.

In the Scandinavian myth, Odin the son of Bur, broke for a season the strength of the great serpent Jörmungard, who, however, eventually swallowed the hero.   Thus was Odin the sun ; and his companions, the other Asir, were more or less sun attributes.   In the case of Egypt the god is Horus (the sun-light), the youthful son of Osiris and Isis, who drives back Typhon to the deserts ; for that country the rising of the Nile is the happy crisis.   Horus is sometimes called Nilus.   Whether the above derivation of the word Typhon be correct or not, which may be doubtful,* that of Horus from the root *Hur* light, connected with the Sanscrit *Ush* to burn (whence also Aurora, etc.,) is certain.   When the great myth became translated to different climates, the evil principle took on different forms of dread.   Water, the

---

* Yet the Hindoo signification of Typhon is "the power of destruction by heat."   In this we have another piece of evidence that both the good and the bad of the fable are referrable to the sun as his varying attributes, and probably describe his particular effects at various portions of the zodiacal year.   The true, or rather the close, meaning of the various accounts is obscured and confused ; firstly, by imperfect knowledge as to the geographical situations where the idea of the zodiac was conceived and developed ; secondly, by the gradual precession of the Equinoxes during the ages which have elapsed since such conception.

rainy season in some countries, the darkness and cold of winter in others, were the Dragon which the Hero-god, the Sun, had to overcome—out of which conflict arose myths innumerable, yet one and the same in essence. Apollo slew the Python, the sunbeams drying up the waters being his arrows; Perseus slew the Dragon, by turning him to stone, which perhaps means that the spring sun dried up the mud of the particular locality where the fable rose. Later, Sigurd slew the Dragon Fafnir. When the Christians found themselves by expediency committed to adopt the form, and to a certain degree the spirit, of heathen beliefs, the Sun *versus* Darkness, or the Spring *versus* Winter myth was a difficulty in very many places. At first the idea was kept up of a material victory over the adverse forces of nature, and we find honourable mention of various bishops and saints, who—by means of which there is little detail, but which may be supposed to be that great monastic beneficence, intelligent drainage—conquered the dragons of flood and fen. It is somewhat odd that the Psalmist attributes to the Deity the victory of breaking the heads of the "dragons in the waters."

Thus St. Romain of Rouen slew there the Dragon Gargouille, which is but the name of a draining-gutter after all, and hence the grotesque waterspouts of our churches are mostly dragons.

St. Martha slew the Dragon Tarasque at Aix-la-chapelle, but that name is derived from *tarir*, to drain. St. Keyne slew the Cornish Dragon, and, to be brief, at least twelve other worthies slew dragons, and doubtless for their respective districts supplied the place of the older myth. Among these, St. George is noteworthy. He is said to have been born at Lydda, in Syria, where his legend awaited the Crusaders, who took him as their patron, bringing him to the west, as the last Christian adoption of a sun-myth idea, to become the patron saint of England. A figure of St. George was a private badge of English kings till the time of the Stuarts. On the · old English angel the combat is between St. Michael and the Dragon, and though St. George is generally shewn mounted, as was also sometimes Horus, the Egyptian deity, he is sometimes represented on foot, like St. Michael. The Dragon is generally the same in the two cases, being the Wyvern or two-legged variety.

Another form of dragon is drake. Certain forms of cannon were called both dragons and drakes. Sometimes the dragon is found termed the Linden-worm, or Lind-drake, in places as widely sundered as Scotland and Germany. It is said this is on account of the dragon dwelling under the linden, a sacred tree, but this is probably only, as yet, half explained.

Perhaps through all time the sun-myth was accompanied by a constant feeling that good and evil were symbolised by the alternation of season. It is to be expected that the feeling would increase and solidify upon the advent of Christianity, for the periodic dragon of heathendom was become the permanent enemy of man, the Devil. The frequent combats between men (and other animals) and the dragons, met among church grotesques, though their models, far remote in an-

tiquity, were representations of sun-myths, would be carved
and read as the ever-continuing fight between good and
evil.   That, however, it is reasonable to see in these Dragon
sculptures direct representatives of the ancient cult, we know
from a fact of date.   The festival of Horus, the Egyptian
deity, was the 23rd of April.   That is the date of St.
George's Day.

Less than the foregoing would scarcely be sufficient to
explain the frequency and significance of the Dragon forms
which crowd our subject.

During the three Rogation days, which took the place
of the Roman processional festivals of the Ambarvalia and
Cerealia, the Dragon was carried as a symbol both in England
and on the continent.   When the Mystery pageantry of
Norwich was swept away, an exception was made in favour of
the Dragon, who, it was ordained, "should come forth and
shew himself as of old."

The Rogation Dragon in France was borne, during the
first two days of the three, before the cross, with a great tail
stuffed with chaff, but on the third day it was carried behind
the cross, with the tail emptied of its contents.   This signified,
it is said, the undisturbed dominion of Satan over the world
during the two days that Christ was in Hell, and his complete
humiliation on the third day.

In some countries the figure of the Dragon, or another
of the Devil, after the procession, was placed on the altar,
then drawn up to the roof, and being allowed to fall was
broken into pieces.

Early Keltic and other pastoral staves end in two Dragons' heads, recalling the caduceus of Mercury and rod of Moses; the Dragon was a Keltic military or tribal ensign. Henry VII. assumed a red dragon as one of the supporters of the royal arms, on account of his Welsh descent; Edward IV. had as one of his numerous badges a black dragon. A dragon issuing from a chalice is the symbol of St. John the Evangelist, an allusion to the dragon of the Apocalypse.

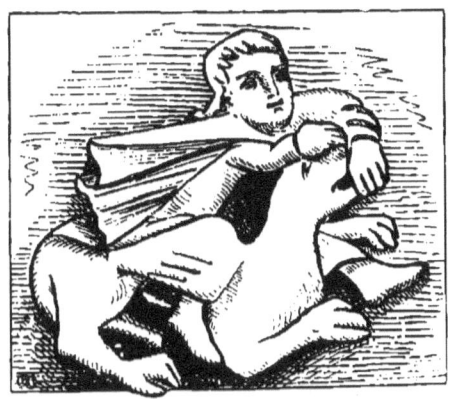

THE SLAYER OF THE DRAGON, IFFLEY.

The Dragon combat here presented is from the south doorway of Iffley Church, near Oxford. In this example of Norman sculpture, the humour intent is more marked than usual. The hero is seated astride the dragon's back, and, grasping its upper and lower jaws, is tearing them asunder. The dragon is rudely enough executed, but the man's face and extremities have good drawing. The cloak flying behind

7

him shew that he has leaped into the quoin of vantage, and recalls the classic. The calm exultation with which the hero seizes his enemy is only equalled by the good-natured amusement which the creature evinces at its own undoing.

We now arrive at a form of the sun-myth which appears to have come down without much interference. The god Horus is alluded to as a child, and in a curious series of carvings the being attacked by a Dragon is a child. It is attempted, and with considerable success, to be represented as of great beauty. The point to explain is the position of the child, rising as it does from a shell. This leads us further into the various contingent mythologies dealing with the Typhon story. Horus (also called Averis, or Orus), was in Egyptian lore also styled Caimis, and is equivalent to Cama, the Cupid of the Hindoos. Typhon (also known as Smu, and as Sambar) is stated to have killed him, and left him in the waters, where Isis restored him to life. That is the account of Herodotus, but Ælian says that Osiris threw Cupid into the ocean, and gave him a shell for his abode. After which he at length killed Typhon.

Hence the shell in the myth-carvings to be found to-day in mediæval Christian churches.

The Greeks represented Cupid, and also Nerites, as living in shells, and, strangely enough, located them on the Red Sea coast, adjacent to the home of the Typhon myth. It is probable that the word *sancha*, a sea-shell, used in this connection, is from *suca*, a cave, a tent; and we may conjecture that there is an allusion to certain dwellers in tents,

THE CHILD AND DRAGON, LINCOLN.

who, coming westward, worked, after a struggle, a political and dynastic revolution, carrying with it great changes in agriculture. This is a conjecture we may, however, readily withdraw in favour of another, that the shell itself is merely a symbol of the ocean, and that Cupid emerging is a figure of the sun rising from the sea at some particular zodiacal period.

Another story kindred to that of Typhon and Horus is that of Sani and Aurva, met in Hindoo literature. They were the sons of Surya, regent of the Sun (Vishnu); Sani was appointed ruler, but becoming a tyrant was deposed, and Aurva reigned in his place. This recalls that one of the names given to Typhon in India was Swarbhánu, "light of heaven," from which it is evident that he is Lucifer, the fallen angel; so that accepting the figurative meaning of all the narratives, we can see even a propriety in the Gothic transmission of these symbolic representations.

It may be added to this that the early conception of Cupid was as the god of Love in a far wider and higher sense than indicated in the later poetical and popular idea. He was not originally considered the son of Venus, whom he preceded in birth. It is scarcely too much to say that he personified the love of a Supreme Unknown for creation; and hence the assumption by Love of the character of a deliverer.

There are other shell deities in mythology. Venus had her shell, and her Northern co-type, Frigga, the wife of the Northern sun-god, Odin, rode in a shell chariot.

The earliest of our examples is the most serious and

precise.   The Dragon is a very bilious and repulsive reptile,
while the child form, thrice repeated in the same carving, has
grace and originality.   This is from Lincoln Minster.

The next is also on a misericorde, and is in Manchester
Cathedral.   Here the shell is different in position, being
upright.   The Child in this has long hair.

The third example is from a misericorde at Beverley
Minster, the series at which place shews strong evidence of
having been executed from the same set of designs as those

DRAGON AND CHILD, BEVERLEY MINSTER.

of Manchester Cathedral, and were carved some twelve years
later.   Many of the subjects are identically the same, but in
this case it will be seen how a meaning may be lost by a
carver's misapprehension.   The shell would not be recogniz-
able without comparison with the other instances, and the
Dragon has become two.   The head of the Child in this
carving appears to be in a close hood, or Puritan infantile cap,
which, as the " foundling cap," survived into this century.
In all the three carvings, the Dragons are of the two-legged

THE CHILD AND DRAGON, MANCHESTER.

kind, which St. George is usually shewn slaying.   It is a little remarkable that the Child's weapon in all three cases is broken away.   The object borne sceptre-wise by the left hand child in the Lincoln carving, is apparently similar to the Egyptian hieroglyphic ʃ, the Greek ϛ, European s.   It may be worth while to suggest that the greatly-discussed collar of ss, worn by the lords chief justices, and others in authority, may have its origin in this hieroglyphic as a symbol of sovereignty,

rather than in any of the arbitrary ascriptions of a mediæval initial.

The weapon is evi-dently a form of the falx, or falcula, for it was with such a one (and here we see further distribution of the myth) that Jupiter wounded Typhon, and such was the instrument with which Perseus slew the sea-dragon : the falx,

THE SLAYING OF THE SNAIL, BEVERLEY MINSTER.

the pruning-hook, sickle or scythe, is an emblem of Saturn, and the oldest representation of it in that connection shew it in simple curved form.   Saturn's sickle became a scythe, and the planet deity thus armed became, on account of the length of his periodical revolution, our familiar figure of Father Time. Osiris, the father of Horus, is styled " the cause of Time." An Egyptian regal coin bears a man cutting corn with a

8

sickle of semi-circular blade.   In many parts of England, the
sickle is spoken of simply as "a hook."

Apparently the carver of the Beverley misericorde was
conscious he had rendered the shell very badly, for in the side
supporter of the carving he had placed, by way of reminder

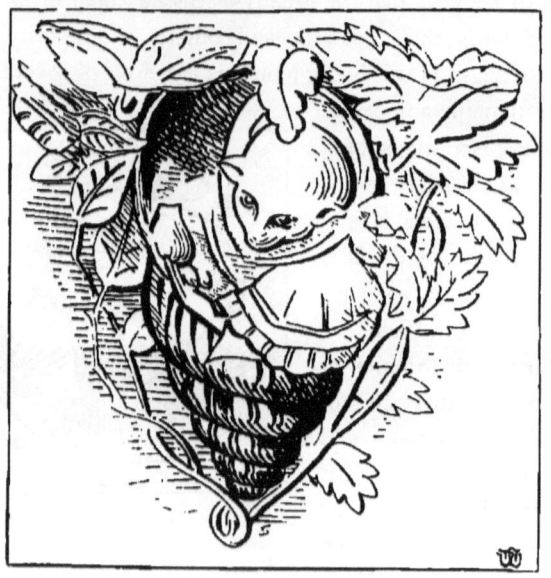

GROTESQUE ON HORNS IN THE SHELL.   THE PALMER FOX EXHIBITING HOLY WATER.
NEW COLLEGE, OXFORD.

as to an attack upon the occupant of a shell, a man in a
fashionable dress, piercing a snail as it approaches him.   In
mediæval carvings, as in many of their explanations, it is
scarcely a step from the sublime to the ridiculous.

One other carving which seems to point to the foregoing

is at New College, Oxford. It is a genuine grotesque, and
may be a satire upon the more serious works. It represents,
seated in the same univalve kind of shell as the others, a fox
or ape in a religious habit, displaying a bottle containing,
perhaps, water from the Holy Land, the Virgin's Milk, or
other wondrous liquid. One of the side carvings is an ape
in a hood bringing a bottle.

Hell's Mouth.

HELL'S MOUTH, HOLY CROSS,
STRATFORD-ON-AVON.

ELL'S Mouth was one of the most popular conceptions of mediæval times. Except so far as concerns the dragon form of the head whose mouth was supposed to be the gates of Hell, the idea appears to be entirely Christian. "Christ's descent into Hell" was a favourite subject of Mystery plays. In the Coventry pageant the "book of words" contained but six verses, in which Hell is styled the "cindery cell." The Chester play is much longer, and is drawn from the Apocryphal Gospel of Nicodemus. This gospel, which has a version in Anglo-Saxon of A.D. 950, is no doubt the source from which is derived a prevalent form of Hell's Mouth in which Christ is represented holding the hand of one of the persons engulped in the infernal jaws. This is seen in a carving on the east window of Dorchester Abbey.

The Mouth is here scarcely that of a dragon, but that of an exceedingly well-studied serpent; for intent and powerful malignity the expression of this fine stone carving would be difficult to surpass. The Descent into Hell is one of a series, on the same window, of incidents in the life of Christ; all are exceedingly quaint, but their distance from the ground improves them in a more than ordinary degree, and their earnest intention prevails over their accidental grotesqueness. The beautiful curves in this viperous head are well worthy of

HELL'S MOUTH, DORCHESTER, OXON.

notice in connection with the remarks upon the artistic qualities of Gothic grotesques.

The verse of the Gospel (xix., 12), explains who the person is. " And [the Lord] taking hold of Adam by his right hand

he ascended from hell and all the saints of God followed
him." The female figure is of course Eve, who is shewn
with Adam in engravings of the subject by Albert Durer
(1512, etc.,) and others. The vision of Piers Ploughman
(*circa* 1362), has particular mention of Adam and Eve
among Satan's captive colony. Satan, on hearing the order
of a voice to open the gates of Hell, exclaims :—

> " Yf he reve me of my ryght he robbeth me by mastrie,
>   For by ryght and reson the reukes [rooks] that be on here
>   Body and soul beth myne both good and ille
>   For he hyms-self hit seide that Syre is of Helle,
>   That Adam and Eve and al hus issue
>   Sholden deye with deol [should die with grief] and here dwell evere
>   Yf thei touchede a tree othr toke ther of an appel."

A MS. volume in the British Museum, of poems written
in the thirty-fourth year of the reign of Henry VI., has "Our
Lady's Song of the Chyld that soked hyr brest," in which
other persons than Adam and Eve are stated to have been
taken out of hell on the same occasion :—

> " Adam and Eve wyth hym he take,
>   Kyng David, Moyses and Salamon
>   And haryed hell every noke,
>   Wythyn hyt left he soulys non."

The belief in the descent in Hell can be traced back to
the second century. The form of Hell as a mouth is much
later.

There is mention of a certain " Mouth of Hell," which in
1437 was used in a Passion play in the plain of Veximiel ;
this Mouth was reported as very well done, for it opened and

shut when the devils required to pass in or out, and it had two large eyes of steel.

The great east window of York Cathedral, the west front and south doorway of Lincoln, and the east side of the altar-screen, Beverley Minster, have representations of the Mouth of Hell. The chancel arch of Southleigh has a large early fresco of the subject, in which two angels, a good and a bad (white and black), are gathering the people out of their graves ; the black spirit is plucking up certain bodies (or souls) with a flesh-hook, and his companions are conveying them to the adjacent Mouth. In a Flemish Book of Hours of the fifteenth century (in the Bodleian Library) there is a representation with very minute details of all the usual adjuncts of the Mouth, and, in addition, several basketsful of children (presumably the unbaptized) brought in on the backs of wolf-like fiends, and on sledges, a common mediæval method of conveyance.

Sackvil mentions Hell as " an hideous hole " that—

"With ougly mouth and griesly jawes doth gape."

Further instances of Hell's Mouth are in the block of the Ludlow ale-wife on a following page.

Satanic Representations.

Q UAINT as are the grotesques derived from the great symbolic Dragon, there is another series of delineations of Evil, which are still more curious. These are the representations of Evil which are to be regarded not so much symbolic as personal. The constant presence of Satan and his satellites on capital and corbel, arcade and misericorde, is to be explained by the exceedingly strong belief in their active participation in mundane affairs in robust physical shapes.

WINCHESTER COLLEGE,
14th century.

It would, perhaps, not seem improper to refer the class of carving instanced by the three cuts, next following, to the Typhon myth. I think, however, a distinction may be drawn between such carvings as represent combat, and such as represent victimization ; the former I would attribute to the myth, the latter to the Christian idea of the torments consequent on sin. At the same time, the victim-carving, generally easily disposed of by

SATAN AND A SOUL, DORCHESTER, OXON.

styling it "Satan and a Soul," is undoubtedly largely influenced by the myth-idea of Typhon (by whatever name known) as a

SATAN AND A SOUL, EWELME, OXON.

seizer, as indicated definitely in one of his general names, Gráha. The figure was naturally one according well with the mediæval understanding of spiritual punishment, and its varieties in carving are numerous enough to furnish an adequate inferno. The Dorchester example is a small boss in the groined ceiling of the sedilia of celebrants; that at Ewelme is a weather-worn parapet-ornament on the south of the choir; the carving at Farnsham is on a misericorde.

REMORSE, YORK.

Not entirely, though in some degree, the two next illustrations support the theory, of punishment rather than conflict, for the others.

The carving in York Cathedral is of a graceful type; there is one closely resembling it at Wells. The Glasgow sketch is from the drawing of a fragment of the cathedral; it is more vivid and ludicrous than the other. A comparison of these two affords a good idea of the excellent in Gothic ornament. The Glasgow carving lacks everything but vigor; the York production, though no exceptional example, has vigor, poetry, and grace.

9

We will now revert to the more personal and "human" aspect of Satan.

REMORSE, GLASGOW.

A writer* in the *Art Journal* some years ago offered excellent general observations upon the ideas of the Evil One found at various periods. He pointed out that the frolicsome character of the mediæval demon was imparted by Christianity, with its forbidden Satan coming into contact with the popular belief in hobgoblins and fairies which were common in the old heathen belief of this island, and so the sterner teaching was tinged by more popular fancies.

There is much truth in this, except that for the hobgoblins and fairies we may very well read ancient deities, for the ultimate effect of Christianity upon Pagan reverence was to turn it into contempt and abhorrence for good and bad deities alike. We can read this in the slender records of ancient worships whose traces are left in language. Thus *Bo* is apparently one of the ancient root-words implying divinity; *Bod*, the goddess of fecundity; *Boivani*, goddess of destruction; *Bolay*, the giant who overcame heaven, earth and hell; *Bouders*, or *Boudons*, the genii guarding Shiva, and *Boroon*, a sea-god, are in Indian mythology. *Bossum* is a good deity of Africa. *Borvo* and *Bormania* were guardians of hot springs, and with *Bouljanus* were gods of old Gaul. *Borr* was the

* Mr. Robert Mann.

SATAN AND A SOUL, DORCHESTER.

father of Odin, and *Bure* was Borr's sister.   The *Bo*-tree
of India is the sacred tree of wisdom.   In Sumatra *boo* is a
root-word meaning good (as in *booroo*).   *Bog* is the Slavonic
for god.   These are given to shew a probable connection
among wide-spread worships.

We are now chiefly concerned with the last instance.
The Slavonic *Bog*, a god, is met in Saxon as a goblin, for the
" boy " who came into the court of King Arthur and laid his
wand upon a boar's head was clearly a " bog " (the Saxon *g*
being exchanged erroneously for *y*, as in *dag's aeg*, day's
eye, etc).   In Welsh, similarly, *Brog* is a goblin, and we have
the evil idea in *bug*.

> " Warwick was a bug that feared us all."
> —*Shakespeare.   Henry IV., v., 2.*

That is " Warwick was a goblin that made us all afraid."
The Boggart is a fairy still believed in by Staffordshire
peasants.   We have yet *bugbear*, as the Russians have *Buka*,
and the Italians *Buggaboo*, of similar meaning.

As with the barbaric gods, so with the classic deities,
who equally supplied material of which to make foul fiends.
Bacchus, with the legs and sprouting horns of a goat, that
haunter of vine-yards, then his fauns constructed on the same
symbolic principle, gave rise to the satyrs.   These, offering in
their form disreputable points for reprobation, were found to
be a sufficiently appropriate symbol of the Devil.   The
reasons of variety in the satyr figure are not far to seek,
beyond the constant tendency of the mediæval artist to vary
form while preserving essence.   Every artist had his idea of

the devil, either drawn from the rich depths of a Gothic
imagination, from the descriptions accumulated by popular
credulity, and most of all from that result of both—the
Devil of the Mystery or Miracle Plays.

The plays were performed by trade gilds.   Every town
had many of these gilds, though several would sometimes
join at the plays ; and even very small villages had both gild
and plays.   There are yet existing some slight traces of
the reputation which obscure villages had in their own
vicinity for their plays, of which Christmas mumming
contains the last tattered relic.   So that, the Devil being a
favourite character in the pieces so widely performed, it is not
surprising to find him equally at home among the works of
the carvers, who, according to the nature of artists of all time,
would doubtless holiday it with the best, and look with more
or less appreciation upon such drama as was set before then.

Where we see Satan as the satyr, he is the rollicking
fiend of the Mystery stage, tempting with sly good-humour,
tormenting with a grim and ferocious joy, or often merely
posturing and capering in a much to be envied height of the
wildest animal spirits.   There is in popular art no trace, so
far as the writer's observation extends, of that lofty sorrow at
man's unworthiness, which has occasionally been attributed to
Satan.

The general feeling is that indicated by the semi-
contemptuous epithets applied to the satyr-idea of "Auld
Clootie" (cloven-footed), and "Auld Hornie," of our Northern
brethren.

Horns were among all ancient nations symbolic of power and dignity. Ancient coinages shew the heads of kings and deities thus adorned. The Goths wore horns. Alexander frequently wore an actual horn to indicate his presumption of divine descent. The head dress of priests was horned on this account. This may point to a pre-historic period when the horned animals were not so much of a prey as we find them in later days; thus the aurochs of Western Europe appears to have been more dreaded by the wild men of its time, than has been, say, the now fast-disappearing bison by

A MAN-GOAT, ALL SOULS, OXFORD.

the North American Indians. On the other hand, the marvellous continuity of nature's designs lead us to recognize that the carnivorous animals must always have had the right to be the symbols of physical power. Therefore, the idea of power, originally conveyed by the horns, is that carried by the possession of riches in the shape of flocks and herds. The pecunia were the means of power, and their horns the symbol of it. With the Egyptians, the ox signified agriculture and subsistence. Pharaoh saw the kine coming out of the Nile because the fertility of Egypt depends upon that river. So that it is easy to see how the ox became the figure of the sun,

and of life. Similar significance attached to the sheep, the
goat, and the ram. Horus is met as "Orus, the Shepherd."
Ammon wore the horns of a ram. Mendes was worshipped
as a goat.

The goat characteristics are well carved on a seat in All
Souls. A goat figure of the thirteenth century at Chichester
has the head of a man with a curious twisted or tied beard,
clutched by one of the hands in which the fore feet terminate.

A CHERISHED BEARD, CHICHESTER.

The clutching of the beard is not uncommon among Gothic
figures, and has doubtless some original on a coin, or other
ancient standard design. At St. Helen's, Abingdon, Berkshire, in different parts of the church, three heads, one being
a king, another a bishop, are shewn grasping or stroking
each his own beard. It is to be remembered that the
stroking of the beard is a well-known Eastern habit.

Of close kindred to the goat form is the bull form. Just
as Ceres symbolized the fecundity of the earth in the matter
of cereals, so Pan was the emblem by which was figured its
productiveness of animal life. Thus Priapus was rendered in

goat form, as the ready type of animal sexual vigor ; but not less familiar in this connection was the bull, and that animal also symbolizes Pan, who became, when superstition grew out of imagery, the protector of cattle in general. An old English superstition was that a piece of horn, hung to the stable or cowhouse key, would protect the animals from night-fright and other ills.   When the pagan Gods were skilfully turned into Christian devils, we find the bull equally with the goat as a Satanic form, and several examples will be seen in the drawings.

The ox, as the symbol of St. Luke, is stated to refer, on account of its cud-chewing, to the eclectic character of this evangelist's gospel.   Irenæus, speaking of the second cherubim of the Revelation, which is the same animal, says the calf signifies the sacerdotal office of Christ ; but the fanciful symbolisms of the fathers and of the Bestiaries are often indifferent guides to original meaning.   It may be that in the ox forms we have astronomical allusions to Taurus, Bacchus, to Diana, or to Pan.   A note on the emblems of the Evangelists follows in the remarks on the combinatory forms met in grotesque art.

Before passing on to consider particular examples of satyr or bull-form fiends, a few words may be said as to another form which, though allied to the dragon-shape embodiments, has the personal character. This is the Serpent. The origin of this appears to be the translation of the word *Nachasch* for serpent in the Biblical account of the momentous Eden episode, a rendering which, without philological certainty, is

10

countenanced by the general presence of the serpent in one
form or another in every system of theology in the world.
Jewish tradition states that the serpent, with beauty of form
and power of flight, had no speech, until in the presence of
Eve he ate of the fruit of the Tree, and so acquired speech,
immediately using the gift to tempt Eve.   Other traditions
say that Nachasch was a camel, and became a serpent by the
curse.   Adam Clarke maintained that Nachasch was a monkey.
The traditional and mystic form of the angels was that of a
serpent. *Seraph* means a fiery serpent.   In Isaiah's vision,
the seraphim are human-headed serpents.   One of the most
remarkable items in the history of worship is the account of
the symbolic serpent erected by Moses, and the subsequent
use of it as an idol until the time of Hezekiah.   In the first satire
of Perseus, he says, "paint two snakes, the place is sacred!"

THE SERPENT, ELY.

The use of the serpent as the
Church symbol of regeneration and
revival of health or life is not common
in carvings.   In these senses it was
used by the Greeks, though chiefly as
the symbol of the Supreme Intellect,
being the special attribute and co-type
of Minerva.   The personal apparition
which confronted Eve is not so in-
frequent, though without much variety.

In a representation of the temptation of Adam and Eve
among the misericordes of Ely, the tree of the knowledge of
good and evil is shewn of a very peculiar shape.   The

serpent, whose coils are difficult to distinguish from the foliage of the tree, has the head of a saturnine Asiatic, who is taking the least possible notice of "our first parents," as they stand eating apples and being ashamed, one on each side of the composition.

A carving in the choir of Chichester Cathedral shews in a double repetition, one half of which is here shewn, the evil head with an attempt at the legendary comeliness, mingled with debased traits, that is artistically very creditable to the sculptor. As though dissatisfied with the amount of beauty he

THE OLD SERPENT, CHICHESTER.
13th century.

had succeeded in imparting to the heads on the serpents, he adds, on the side-pieces of the carving, two other heads of females in eastern head-dresses, to which he has imparted a

DEMURENESS MEDITATING MISCHIEF.
DEUTCHO-EGYPTIAN MASK,
CHICHESTER.

demure Dutch beauty, due perhaps to his own nationality. Human-headed serpents are in carvings at Norwich and at Bridge, Kent.

With regard to Satan's status as an angel, a considerable number of representations of him are to be found, in which he conforms to a prevalent mediæval idea as to the plumage of the spirit race. Angels are found clothed entirely with feathers, as repeated

some scores of times in the memorial chapel, at Ewelme, of
Alice, Duchess of Suffolk, grand-daughter of Chaucer, who
died in 1475. The annexed block shews a small archangel

which surmounts the font canopy, and is of
the same character as the chapel angels.
At All·Souls, Oxford, is a carving of a
warrior-visaged person wearing a morion,
and armed with a falchion and buckler.
He is clad in feathers only, appearing to be
flying downward, and is either a representation of St. Michael or Lucifer.

ANGEL, EWELME.

Satan is often similarly treated. Loki,
the tempter of the Scandinavian Eden, who
was ordered to seek the lost Idun he had deceived, had

ST. MICHAEL, ALL SOULS, OXFORD.

to go forth clad in borrowed garments of falcon's feathers with wings.   When the pageant at the Setting of the Midsummer Watch at Chester was forbidden by the Mayor, in 1599, one of the prohibited figures was "the Devil and his Feathers."

There may be a connection between the final punishment of Loki and the idea embodied in the carvings mentioned above as being at, among other places, Wells, York, and Glasgow, and which have been considered as conceptions of Remorse.   Loki was condemned to be fastened to a rock to helplessly endure the eternal dropping upon his brow of poison from the jaws of a serpent ; only that there is neither in these carvings, nor any others noted to the present, any indication of the presence of the ministering woman-spirit who for even the fiend Loki stood by to catch the death-drops in a cup of mercy.

The Devil and the Vices.

RECORDING IMP,
ST. KATHERINE'S, REGENT'S PARK.
(*Initial added*).

AVING examined the various lower forms given by man to his great enemy, and now noting that to such forms may be added the human figure in whole or part, we will next take in review a few of the sins which bring erring humanity into the clutches of Satan; for we find some of the most grotesque of antique carvings devoted to representation of what may be called the finale of the Sinner's Progress. These are probably largely derived from the Mystery Plays; for the moral teaching has the same direct soundness. The ideas are often jocosely put, but the principle is one of mere retribution. The Devil cannot hurt the Saint and he pays out to the Wicked the exact price of his wrong-doing. Thus in nearly all of what may be termed the Sin series there is a Recording Imp who bears a tablet or scroll, on which we are to suppose the evil commissions and omissions of the sinner are duly entered, entitling the fiend to take possession. This reminds of the Egyptian Mercury, Thoth, who recorded upon his tablets the actions of men, in order that at the Judgment there might be proper evidence.

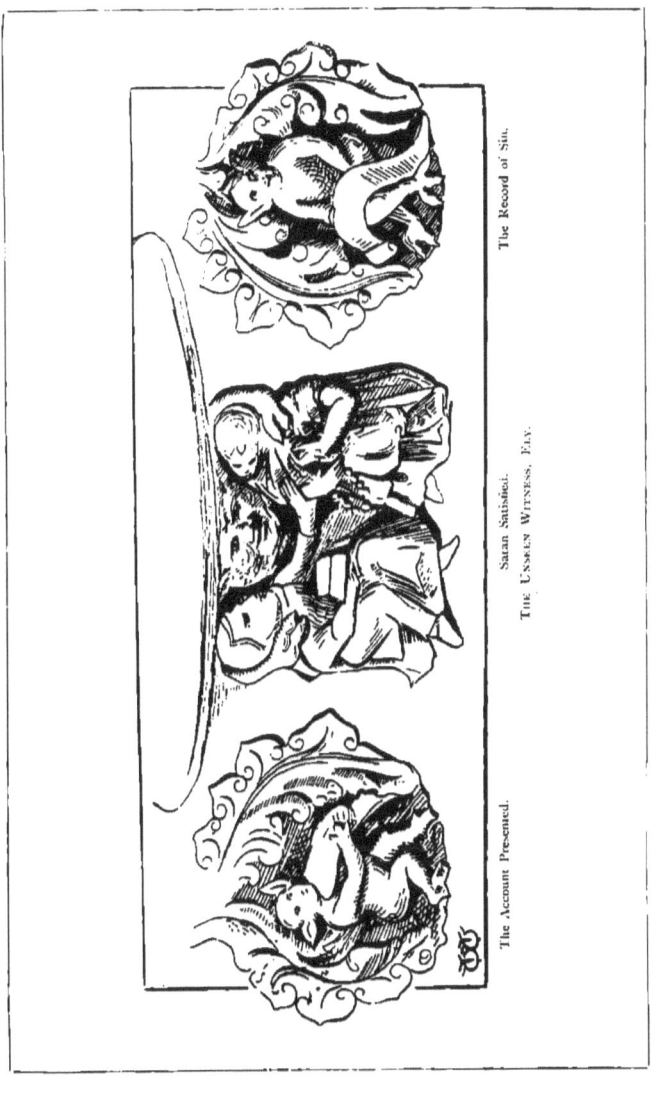

The Account Presented. Satan Satisfied. The Record of Sin.

THE UNSEEN WITNESS, ETC.

There is a series of carvings, examplified at Ely, New College, Oxford, St. Katherine's (removed from near the Tower to the Regent's Park) and Gayton, which have Satan encouraging or embracing two figures apparently engaged in conversation. I have placed these among the Sins, for though no very particular explanation is forthcoming as to the meaning of the group, it is clear that the two human beings are engaged in some occupation highly agreeable to the fiend. This evidently has a connection with the monkish story told of St. Britius. One day, while St. Martin was saying mass, Britius, who was officiating as deacon, saw the devil behind the altar, writing on a slip of parchment "as long as a proctor's bill" the sins which the congregation were then and there committing. The people, both men and women, appear to have been doing many other things besides listening to St. Martin, for the devil soon filled his scroll on both sides. Thus far our carvings.

The story goes further, and states that the devil, having further sins to record, but no further space on which to write them, attempted to stretch the parchment with teeth and claws, which, however, broke the record, the devil falling back against a wall. The story then betrays itself. Britius laughed loudly, whereat St. Martin, highly displeased, demanded the reason, when Britius told him what he had seen, which relation the other saint accepted as being true.

This story is one of a class common among mediæval pulpit anecdotes. It cannot well be considered that the carvings arose from the story, nor the story from the carvings.

11

Probably both arose from something else, accounting for the
number of sinners being uniformly two, and for the attitude
of the fiend in each case being so similar. With regard to
the latter I must leave the matter as it is.

I venture, as to the signification of the two figures,
to make a suggestion to stand good until a better be
found. In the Mystery Play entitled the "Trial of Mary and
Joseph (Cotton MS., Pageant xiv., amplified out of the
Apocryphal New Testament, *Protevan*, xi.), the story runs
that Mary and Joseph, particularly the former, are defamed
by two Slanderers. The Bishop sends his Summoner for the
two accused persons, and orders that they drink the water of
vengeance "which is for trial," a kind of miraculous ordeal by
poison. Joseph drinks and is unhurt ; Mary likewise and is
declared a pure maid in spite of facts. One of the Slanderers
declares that the drink has been changed because the Virgin
was of the High Priest's kindred, upon which the Slanderer
is himself ordered to drink what is left in the cup. Doing
so he instantly becomes frantic. All ask pardon of Mary for
their suspicions, and, that being granted, the play is ended.

Now the play commences with the meeting of the Two
Slanderers. A brief extract or two will shew their method.

1ST. DETRACTOR.—To reyse blawthyr is al my lay,
   Bakbyter is my brother of blood .
  Dede he ought come hethyr in al this day
   Now wolde God that he were here,
  And, by my trewth, I dare well say
  That if we twcyn to gethyr apere
  Mor slawndyr we t[w]o schal a rere

With in an howre thorwe outh this town,
Than evyr ther was this thouwsand yer,
Now, be my trewth, I have a sight
Evyn of my brother . . . Welcome

2ND DETRACTOR.—I am ful glad we met this day.

1ST DETRACTOR.—Telle all these pepyl [the audience] what is yoᵣ name—

2ND DETRACTOR.—I am Bakbyter, that spyllyth all game,
             Both hyd and known in many a place.

Then they fall to, and in terms of some wit and much freedom describe the physical condition of she who was "calde mayd Mary."

The Two Slanderers in this play are undoubtedly men, for each styles the other "brother." Yet there are words in their dialogue, not suited to these pages, which could properly only be used by women. As in at least one of the carvings the sinners are women, if my hypothesis has any correctness there must be some other form of the story in which the detractors are female.

A BACKBITER, ST. KATHERINE'S.

It is to be noted, also, that the play from which I have quoted has no mention of the devil.

Years before I met with the play of the trial of Joseph and Mary, I considered that the sin of the Two might be scandal, and put down a curious carving adjoining the St. Katherine group as a reference to it, and suggested it might be a humorous rendering of a Backbiter. This is shewn in the accompanying block. It was therefore agreeable to find one of the Mystery detractors actually named Backbiter. Against that it may be mentioned that the composite figure with a head at the rear is not unique. At Rothwell, Northampton-shire, is a dragon attempt, rude though probably of late fifteenth century work, with a similar head in the same anatomical direction; this is not connected with anything that can be considered bearing upon the subject of the Mystery, unless the heads on the same misericorde are meant to be those of Jews.

A BACKBITER, ROTHWELL, NORTHANTS.

The example at Ely shews the fiend closely embracing the two sinners who are evidently in the height of an impressive conversation. One figure has a book on its knee, the other is telling the beads of a rosary. At the sides are two imps of a somewhat Robin Goodfellow-like character, each bearing a scroll with the account of the misdeeds of the sinners, and which we may presume are the warrants by which Satan is entitled to seize his prey. He is the picture of jovial good-nature.

New College, Oxford, has a misericorde of the subject in which the figures, female in appearance, are seated in a sort of box. This reminds us of Baldini and Boticelli's picture of Hell, which is divided into various ovens for different vices. That may be the idea here, or perhaps the object is a coffin and is used to emphasize what the wages of sin are. They, like the two sinners of Ely, are in animated conversation. Satan here is of a bull-headed form with wings rather like those of a butterfly. These are of the end of the fifteenth century.

THE UNSEEN WITNESS, NEW COLLEGE, OXFORD.

There are foreign carvings described by Mr. Evans as being of the devil taking notes of the idle words of two women during mass. This is, perhaps, the simple meaning of all this series, and an evidence of the resentment of ecclesiastics against the irreverent. There is considerable evidence that religious service was scarcely a solemn thing in mediæval times. If this is the signification the box

arrangement described above may be some sort of early
pew.

The next example, from St. Katherine's (lately) by the
Tower, has the fiend in a fashionable slashed suit. The
ladies here are only in bust, and though of demurely
interested expression they have not that rapport and
animation which distinguish the two previously noticed.
Satan does not embrace them, but stands behind with legs

THE UNSEEN WITNESS, ST. KATHERINE'S.

outstretched and hands, or rather claws, on knees, ready to
clutch them at the proper moment.

At Gayton, Northants, is a further curious instance of
this group. The two Sinners are in this case unquestionably
males, and, but for the coincidence with the preceding
examples, the men might have been supposed to have been
engaged in some game of chance. It will be observed that
the one to the right has a rosary as in the first-named carving.

Satan here is well clothed in feathers, and in his left wing is the head of what is probably one of the instruments of torture awaiting the very much overshadowed victims. It is a kind of rake or flesh-hook, with three sharp, hooked teeth; perhaps a figure of the tongue of a slanderer, materialized for his own subsequent scarification; it may be added as a kind of satanic badge. Satan bears on his right arm a leaf-shaped shield.

THE UNSEEN WITNESS, GAYTON, NORTHANTS.

The vice next to be regarded is Avarice. In a misericorde at Beverley Minster we have three scenes from the history of the Devil. One gives us the avaricious man bending before his coffers. He has taken out a coin; if we read aright his contemplative and affectionate look, it is gold.

Hidden behind the chest behold Satan, one of whose bullock
horns is visible as he lurks out of the miser's sight, grinning
to think how surely the victim is his.

At the opposite end of the carving is the other extreme,
Gluttony. A man is drinking out of a huge flask, which he
holds in his right hand, while in the other he grasps a ham

THE DEVIL AND THE MISER, BEVERLEY MINSTER.

(or is it not impossible that this is a second bottle). In this
the devil is likewise present; he is apparently desperately
anxious the victim should have enough.

Between these two reliefs appears Satan seizing a naked
soul. In the original all that remains of the Devil's head is

SATAN AND A SOUL, BEVERLEY MINSTER

the outline and one horn ; of the soul's head there remains
only the outline ; the two faces I have ventured to supply,
also the fore-arm of the Devil.   The fiend is here again
presented with the attributes of a bullock, rather than a goat.
Satan has had placed on his abdomen a mask or face, a
somewhat common method of adding to the startling effect
of his boisterous personality.   The fine rush which the fiend

THE DEVIL AND THE GLUTTON, BEVERLEY MINSTER.

is making upon the soul, and the shrinking horror of the
latter, are exceedingly well rendered.   The moral is, we
may suppose, that the sinners on either side will come to
the same bad end.

Among the seat-carvings of Henry VII's. Chapel,
Westminster Abbey, we have the vice of Avarice more

fully treated, there being two carvings devoted to the subject. In the first we see a monk suddenly seized by a quaint and curious devil (to whom I have supplied his right fore-arm). The monk, horror-stricken, yet angry, has dropped his bag of sovereigns, or nobles, and the coins fall out. He would escape if he could, but the claws of the fiend have him fast.

In the companion carving we have the incident—and the monk—carried a little further. The devil has picked him up, thrown him down along his conveniently horizontal back, and strides on with him through a wild place of rocks and trees,

DISMAY, WESTMINSTER.

holding what appears to be a flaming torch, which he also uses as a staff. The monk has managed to gather up his dearly-loved bag of money, and is frantically clutching at the rocks as he is swiftly borne along. Satan in the first carving has rather a benevolent human face, in the second a debased beast face, unknown to natural history. There is no explanation of how Sathanus has disposed in the second scene of the graceful dragon wings he wears in the first. It is probable that two of the Italians who carved this set each took the same subject, and we have here their respective renderings. I mention with diffidence that if the mild and timorous face of Bishop Alcock (which may be seen at Jesus College, Cambridge), the architect of this part of the abbey, could be supposed to have unfortunately borne at any time the expressions upon either

THE OVERTAKING OF AVARICE, WESTMINSTER.

THE TAKING OF THE AVARICIOUS, WESTMINSTER.

of these two representations of the monk, the likeness would, in my opinion, be rather striking.

On the side carving of the carrying-away scene is shewn a woman, dismayed at the sight. On the opposite side a fiend is welcoming the monk with beat of drum, just as we shall see the ale-wife saluted with the drone of the bagpipes.

DEMONIACAL DRUMMER, WESTMINSTER.

A carving at St. Mary's Minster, Isle of Thanet, has the devil looking out with a vexed frown from between the horns of a lofty head-dress, which is on a lady's head. Whether this be a rendering of the dishonest ale-wife, or a separate warning against the vice of Vanity, cannot well be decided.

VANITY, ST. MARY'S MINSTER.

There was a popular opinion at one time that the bulk of church carvings were jokes at the expense of clergy, probably largely because every hood was thought to be a cowl. There

13

is, however, no doubt as to the carving here presented.   It
may represent the consecration of a bishop.   The presence of
Satan dominating both the individuals, and pulling forward

HYPOCRISY, NEW COLLEGE, OXFORD.

the cowl of the seated figure, appears to declare that this is
to illustrate the vice of Hypocrisy.   It is at New College,
Oxford.

Ale and the Ale-wife.

THE JOLLY TAPSTER,
LUDLOW.

LE, good old ale, has formed the burden of more songs and satires ancient and modern, than will ever be brought together. Ale was the staple beverage for morning, noon, and evening meals. It is probable that swollen as is the beer portion of the Budget, the consumption of ale, man for man, is much less than that of any mediæval time. The records of all the authoritative bodies who dealt with the liquor traffic of the olden time are crowded with rules and regulations that plainly demonstrate not only the universal prevalence of beer drinking in a proper and domestic degree, but also the constant growing abuse of the sale of the liquor. In the reign of Elizabeth the evils of the tavern had become so notorious, that in some places women were forbidden to keep ale-houses.

As far back as A.D. 794, ale-houses had become an institution, for we find the orders passed at the Council of Frankfort in that year included one by which ecclesiastics and monks were forbidden to drink in an ale-house. St. Adrian was the patron of brewers.

In some boroughs (Hull may be given as an instance) in the fifteenth century, the Mayor was not allowed to keep a tavern in his year of office. Brewers and tavern keepers, with many nice distinctions of grade among them, were duly licensed and supervised, various penalties meeting attempts at illicit trade. The quality of ale was also an object of solicitude, and an official, called the ale-taster, was in nearly every centre of population made responsible for the due strength and purity of the national beverage. It was customary in some places in the fifteenth century for the ale-taster to be remunerated by a payment of 4d. a year from each brewer.

It has to be remembered ale was drunk at the meals at which we now use tea, coffee, and cocoa ; it will be interesting to glance at an instance of the rate at which it was consumed. At the Hospital of St. Cross, founded in 1132, at Winchester, thirteen "impotent" men had each a daily allowance of a gallon and a half of good small beer, with more on holidays ; this was afterwards reduced to three quarts with some two quarts extra for holidays. The porter at the gate had only three quarts to give away to beggars. There was great idea of continuity at this establishment ; even in 1836 there was spent £133 5s. for malt and hops for the year's brewing. The happy thirteen had each yet three quarts every day as well as a jack (say four gallons) extra among them on holidays, with 4s. for beer money. Two gallons of beer were also daily dispensed at the gate at the rate of a horn of not quite half a pint to each applicant.

Ale, no more than other things, could be kept out of church. A carving at Wellingborough, Northamptonshire, shews us an interview between a would-be customer on the one part and an ale-wife on the other part. There is, in a list of imaginary names in an epilogue or "gagging"

LETTICE LITTLETRUST AND A SIMPLE SIMON. WELLINGBOROUGH, *14th century.*

summons to a miracle play, mention of one Letyce Lytyl-trust, whom surely we see above. Evidently the man is better known than trusted, and while a generous supply of the desired refreshment is "on reserve" in a dear old jug, some intimation has been made that cash is required; he, like one Simon on a similar occasion, has not a penny, and with

one hand dipped into his empty pocket, he scratches his head
with the other.   His good-natured perplexity contrasts well
with the indifferent tradeswoman-like air of the ale-wife, who
while she rests the jug upon a bench, does not relinquish the
handle.   He is saying to himself, "Nay, marry, an I wanted
a cup o' ale aforetime I was ever served.   A thirsty morn is
this.   I know not what to say to t' jade;" while she is
muttering, "An he wipe off the chalk ahint the door even, he
might drink and welcome, sorry rogue tho' he be.   But no
use to cry pay when t' barrel be empty."

At Edgeware in 1558, an innkeeper, was fined for selling
a pint and a half of ale at an exorbitant price, namely, one
penny.   A quart was everywhere the proper quantity, and
that of the strongest; small ale sold at one penny for two
quarts.   With regard to the then higher value of money,
however, the prices may be considered to be about the same
as at present, and the same may be said of many commodities
which appear in records at low figures.

Of an earlier date is the tapster of the initial block, from
Ludlow, who furnishes a comfortable idea of a congenial, and
to judge from his pouch, a profitable occupation.   It is to be
presumed the smallness of the barrel as compared with that of
the jug—probably of copper, and dazzlingly bright—was the
artist's means of getting its full outline within the picture, and
not an indication of the relations of supply and demand.

Alas for the final fate of the dishonest woman who could
cheat men in the important matter of ale!   At Ludlow we are
shewn such a one, stripped of all but the head dress and neck-

lace of her vanity, and carried ignominiously and indecorously
to Hell's Mouth on the shoulders of a stalwart demon (whose
head is supplied in the block). In her hand, and partaking
of her own reverse, she bears the hooped tankard with which
she defrauded her customers. It is the measure of her woe.
The demon thus loaded with mischief is met by another,
armed with the bagpipes. With hilarious air and fiendish

THE END OF THE ALE-WIFE, LUDLOW.

grin he welcomes the latest addition to the collection of
evil-doers within. To the right are the usual gaping jaws of
Hell's Mouth, into which are disappearing two nude females,
who, we may suppose, are other ale-wifes not more meritorious
than the lady of the horned head dress. To the left is the
Recording Imp.

There is allusion in a copy of the Chester Mystery of

Christ's Descent into Hell, among the Harleian MSS., to an ale-wife of Chester, which doubtless suggested this carving. This lady, a little-trust and a cheater in her day, laments having to dwell among the fiends; she endeavours to propitiate one of them by addressing him as "My Sweet Master

THE FEMALE DRAWER, ALL SOULS, OXFORD.

Sir Sattanas," who returns the compliment by calling her his "dear darling."   She announces that :—

"Some tyme I was a tavernere,
A gentill gossipe and a tapstere,
Of wyne and ale a trustie brewer,
    Which wo hath me wroughte.
Of cannes I kepte no trewe measuer
My cuppes I soulde at my pleasuer,
Deceaving manye a creature,
    Tho' my ale were naughte."

The Devil then delivers a short speech, which is one of the earliest temperance addresses on record. He says :—

> " Welckome, dere ladye, I shall thee wedd,
> For many a heavye and droncken head
> Cause of thy ale were broughte to bed
> Farre worse than anye beaste."

There is an old saying "pull Devil, pull Baker" connected with the representation of a baker who sold his bread short of weight, and was carried to the lower regions in his own basket ; the ale-wife, of our carving, however,

A HORN OF ALE, ELY.

does not appear to have retained any power of resistance, however slight or ineffectual.

At All Souls, Oxford, there is a good carving of a woman drawing ale. It is not, apparently, the ale-wife herself, but the maid sent down into the cellar. The maid, perhaps after a good draught of the brew, seems to be blowing a whistle to convey, to the probably listening ears of her mistress upstairs, the impression that the jug has not received any improper attention from her. The artful expression of the ale-loving maid lends countenance to the conjecture that the precaution has not been entirely efficacious. It is to this day a jocular expression in Oxfordshire, and perhaps elsewhere, " You had better whistle while you are drawing that beer."

A carving at Ely represents Pan as an appreciative imbiber from a veritable horn of ale.

14

Satires without Satan.

HERE are numbers of grotesques which are satires evidently aimed at sins, but which have not the visible attendance of the evil one himself.

Among these must be included a curious carving from Swine, in Holderness. The priory of Swine was a Cistercian nunnery of fifteen sisters and a prioress. Mr. Thomas Blashill states, "There were, however, two canons at least, to assist in the offices of religion, who did not refrain from meddling in secular affairs." * There was also a small community of lay-brethren.

THE SLUMBERING PRIEST,
NEW COLLEGE, OXFORD.

The female in the centre of the carving is a nun; her hood is drawn partly over her face, so that only one eye is fully visible, but with the other eye she is executing a well-known movement of but momentary duration. The two ugly animals between which she peers are intended for hares, a symbol of libidinousness, as well as of timidity.

Another carving in the same chancel may be in derision of some official of the papal court, which, in the thirteenth century, on an occasion of the contumacy of the nuns in

* " Sutton-in-Holderness."

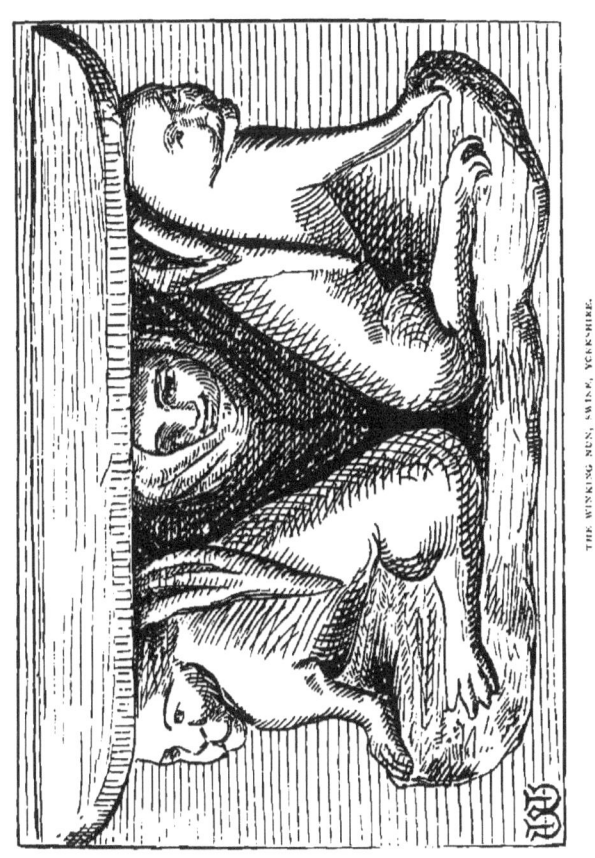

refusing to pay certain tithes, caused the church, with that adjoining, of the lay brethren, to be closed. The nuns defied all authority, broke open the chapels, and in general during

A PAPAL MONSTER, SWINE, YORKSHIRE.

the long contest acted in a curiously ungovernable, irresponsible manner.

At Bishop's Stortford, Hertfordshire, are some miseri-

cordes, which, says Miss Phipson, are stated to have originally belonged to Old St. Paul's. Among them is the annexed subject. The wicked expression of the face, and the general incorrectness of the composition, are a historical evidence of

IMPUDENCE, BISHOP'S STORTFORD, HERTFORDSHIRE.

indecorum akin to the gestures of the Beverley carvers.

From the fine choir carvings of Westminster Abbey yet another example is given. It is one in which the spirit of the old *Comptes a Plaisance* is well illustrated. A well-clad man, suggesting Falstaff in his prime, is seated with a lady among luxurious foliage.   His arm is right round his companion's waist, while his left hand dips into his capacious and apparently well-lined pouch, or gipciere.   He has been styled a merchant. He is manifestly making a bargain.   The lady is evidently a daughter of the hireling (*hirudo !*), and is crying, "Give, give."   In spite of this being the work of an Italian artist,

A QUESTION OF PRICE, WESTMINSTER ABBEY.

the artistic feeling about it would seem to recall slightly the lines of Holbein.

The small carving to the right of the above is a highly-elate pig, playing the pipe.   This is shewn in a short chapter hereafter given on Animal Musicians.   The initial at the head of this chapter is illustrated with the "slumbering priest," the carving of whom is at the right of that of the 'Unseen

Witness,' drawn on page 85. This doubtless implies that some portion of the sin of the people was to be attributed to the indifference of the clergy. Balancing this, there is in the original carving an aged person kneeling, and, supported by a crutch, counting her beads.

In a subsequent chapter (on Compound Forms in Gothic) the harpy is mentioned, and shewn to be a not uncommon subject of church art, either as from the malignant classic form which symbolized fierce bad weather, or as the more beneficient though not unsimilar figure which was the symbol of Athor, the Egyptian Venus. A Winchester example which might seem in place among the remarks on the Compounds, is included here, as it is evidently intended to embody a sin. It serves to show that a modern use of the word harpy was well understood in mediæval times. The design is simple, the vulture wings being made to take the position of the hair of the woman head. She lies in wait spider-wise, her great claws in readiness for the prey ; and is evidently a character-sketch of a coarse, insatiable daughter of the horse-leech.

THE HARPY IN WAIT, WINCHESTER.

Scriptural Illustrations.

ADAM AND EVE,
BEVERLEY MINSTER.

MYSTERY Plays, we have seen, drew upon the Apocryphal New Testament for subjects, but it has simply happened that the examples of vice carvings illustrate those writings, for Mystery Plays were in general founded upon the canonical scriptures. There are many carvings which have Biblical incidents for their subject, but it is often impossible to say whether the text were the sole material of the designer, or whether his ideas were formed by representations he had seen on the Mystery stage. It may be presumed that the effect would not be greatly different in one case from the other.

The story of Jonah furnishes a subject for two misericordes in Ripon Cathedral. One is in the frontispiece of this volume. In the first the prophet is being pushed by three men unceremoniously over the side of the vessel which has the usual mediæval characteristics, and, in which, plainly, there is no room for a fourth person. The ship is riding easily on by no means tumultuous waves, out of which protrudes the head of the great fish. The fish and Jonah appear to regard the situation with equal complacency.

In the sequel carving Jonah is shewn being cast out by

THE STORY OF JONAH.   THE CASTING OUT.

the fish, of which, as in the other, the head only is visible. The monster of the deep has altered its appearance slightly during the period of Jonah's incarceration, its square upper teeth having become pointed. The prophet is represented kneeling among the teeth, apparently offering up thanks for his deliverance. The sea is bounded by a rocky shore on which stand trees of the well-known grotesque type in which they are excellent fir-cones.

These two carvings are of somewhat special interest, as their precise origin is known. They are both exceedingly close copies of engravings in the Biblia Pauperum, or Poor Man's Bible, otherwise called "Speculum Humanæ Salvationis," or the Mirror of Human Salvation. Other Biblical subjects in the Ripon Series of Misericordes are from the same source. Did the Sculptor or Sculptors of the series fall short of subjects, or were their eyes caught by the definite outlines of the prints in the "Picture Bible" as it lay chained in the Minster?

The Adoration, in a carving in the choir of Worcester, comes under the head of unintentional grotesques. It is a proof that though the manipulative skill of the artist may be great, that may only accentuate his failure to grasp the true spirit of a subject; and render what might have been only a piece of simplicity, into an elaborate grotesque. The common-place, ugly features—where not broken away—the repeated attitudes and the symmetric arrangement join to defeat the artist's aim. Add to those the anachronisms, the ancient Eastern rulers in Edward III. crowns and gowns,

15

seated beneath late Gothic Decorated Arches offering gifts,
and the absurdity is nearly complete. It is difficult to quite
understand the presence of the lady with gnarled features, on
the left, bearing the swathed infant (headless) which seems to
demonstrate that this was carved by a foreigner, or was from
a foreign source ; for though swathing was practised to some
extent in England, I can only find that in Holland, Germany,
etc., and more especially in Italy, the children were swathed
to this extent, in the complete mummy fashion styled
"bambino."

Perhaps the reason of the two figures right and left was
that the artist went with the artistic tide in representing the
recently-born infant as a strapping boy of four or five ; yet his
common-sense telling him that was a violation of fact he put the
other figure in with the strapped infant to show what—in his
own private opinion—the child would really be like at the time.

We might have supposed it to be St. John, but he was
older and not younger than the Divine Child. In the
Scandinavian mythology, Vali, the New Year, is represented
as a child in swaddling clothes.

The Scriptural subjects in carved work may be compared
with the wall paintings which in a few instances have survived
the reforming zeal of bygone white-washing churchwardens.
The comparison is infinitely to the advantage of the carvings.
These paintings are in distemper and were the humble inartistic
precursors of noble frescoes in the continental fanes, but which
had in England no development. To what extent there was
merit in the mural decoration of the English cathedrals cannot

ADORATION OF THE MAGI, WORCHES-TER.

well be stated.   Such examples, as in a few churches are left
to us, are simply curiosities.   Though changing with the
styles they are more crude than the sculptures, and the
modern eye in search of the grotesque, finds here compositions
infinitely more excruciatingly imbecile than in any other
department of art-work of pretension.

     At the same time when they are considered in conjunction

BAPTISMAL SCENE, GUILDFORD.

with the most perfect of the paintings of their period they are
by no means so low in the scale of merit as at the first thought
might be supposed.

     Outside the present purpose of looking at them as
unintentional grotesques they are very valuable specimens of
the English art of painting of dates which have, except in
illuminations, no other examples.

Those of St. Mary's, Guildford, are very quaint. The
first selected from the series is a representation of Christ
attending the ministration of St. John the Baptist. St. John
has apparently taken down to the river bank a classic font, in
which is seated a convert. The Baptist himself, wearing a
Phrygian cap (probably Saxon), is turning away from the
figures of Christ and the man in the font, and is apparently

CASTING OUT OF DEVILS, GUILDFORD.

addressing a company which does not appear in the picture.
Just as the font was put in to make the idea of baptism easily
understood, so, we may suppose, the curious buttons on
thongs, or whatever they are, were shewn attached to St.
John's wrist, to indicate that he is speaking of the "shoe-
latchets." The waters and bank of the Jordan are indicated
in a few lines.

The other selection is still more bizarre. It evidently portrays Christ casting out devils. The chief point of interest in this painting is the original conception of the devils. Anything more vicious, degraded, and abhorrent, it would be difficult to produce in so few lines. Roughly speaking, they are a compound of the hawk, the hog, and the monkey; this curious illustration is an excellent pendant to the marks made upon early Satanic depictions on a previous page. The faces are Saxon, except in the case of the man with the sword, who is a distinct attempt at a Roman. The artist had evidently in his mind one who was set in authority.

The churches of the Midlands are rich in wall-paintings.

A fine example is in North Stoke Church, Oxfordshire, which has two Scriptural subjects, a series of angelic figures, and several other figures, etc., only fragmentally visible. They were all found accidentally under thick coats of white-wash. It may be doubted whether they were ever finished. The two Biblical subjects are "Christ betrayed in the Garden," and "Christ before Pilate." Christ is a small apparently blind-folded figure, of which only the head and one shoulder remains. Pilot is the Saxon lord, posing as the seated figure of legal authority, poising a hiltless sword in his right hand. The figure addressing Pilate is apparently a Roman (Saxon) official; his hand is very large, but there is a simple force about his drawing. The fourth figure in a mitre is doubtless meant for a Jewish priest, and he has a nasty, clamorous look. Pilate, unfortunately, has no pupils to his eyes, but his general appearance is as though he was expostulating with the priest.

There is a carol, printed in 1820, which has a woodcut of the subject not less rude and not less of an anachronism than this : but what is curious, as illustrating the main theory of the present volume—the tenacity with which form is adhered to in unconscious art—is that the disposition of the figures is exactly the same in both pictures. Where the Saxon lord is seated, imagine a bearded magistrate, at a sort of Georgian quarter-sessions bench, with panelled front. For the simple Saxon, with vandyked shirt, suppose a Roman half-soldier, half-village-policeman. Then comes the figure of Christ, with the head much lower than those of the others because he is nearer. Lastly, there is an incomplete figure behind.

In this case the perfect correspondence may be mere coincidence ; it is difficult to explain otherwise. The design, however, is the same, only the Anglo-Norman filled in his detail from his observation of a manorial court, the Moorfield engraver from his knowledge of Bow Street police-court.

To conclude, although these paintings are ludicrous in the extreme, the artists, who had no easy task, were absolutely serious, and their works, divested of the comic aspect conferred by haste and manipulative incompetence, are marked by bold impressiveness.

The initial to this chapter is from one of a series of similar ornaments on the parapet of the south side of the nave of Beverley Minster ; it illustrates the toilsome nature of the later portion of Adam's life.

Masks and Faces.

FOLIATE MASK,
THE CHOIR, BEVERLEY MINSTER.

HE merriest, oddest, most ill-assorted company in the world meet together in the masks and faces of Gothic ornament. Space could always be found for a head, and skill to execute it. Yet though the variety is immense, the faces of Gothic art will be found to classify themselves very definitely.

Perhaps the most prevalent type is the classic mask with leaves issuing from the mouth. This may be an idea of the

FOLIATE MASK, DORCHESTER, OXON.

16

mask which every player in the ancient drama wore, displayed
as an ornament with laurel, bay, oak, ivy, or what not, inserted
in the mouth, because it was pierced for speaking through,

and the only aperture in which
the decorative branches could be
inserted.   Or seeds might germ-
inate in sculptured masks and so
have suggested the idea.   Masks
were hung in vineyards, etc.

A mask above the internal
tower-doorway in the Lady Chapel
of Dorchester Abbey has a close

FOLIATE MASK, ST. MARY'S MINSTER,
ISLE OF THANET.

resemblance to the classic mask in the protruding lips, which,
for the conveying of the voice for the great distance necessary
in the arrangement of the ancient theatres, were often shaped

FOLIATE MASK, BEVERLEY MINSTER.

like a shallow speaking-trumpet.   The leaves appear to be
the vine, and so the head, perhaps, that of Bacchus.   Between
the eyebrows will be noticed an angular projection.   This

is probably explained by a mask in a misericorde in St.
Mary's Minster, in which some object, perhaps the nasal of
a helmet, comes down the middle of the forehead. The

INDIAN MASK, ST. MARY'S, BEVERLEY.

leaves in this case appear to be oak, which is, indeed, the
prevailing tree used for the purpose.

Occasionally a mask with leaves has the tongue protruding.

LATE ITALIAN FOLIATE MASK, WESTMINSTER.

Perhaps one of the most remarkable masks in Gothic is
on another misericorde in the same town, but in St. Mary's
Church ; in which the features, the head-dress, the treatment
of the ears, are all Indian, while the leaves are those of the

palm.   This is, perhaps, unique as an instance of Gothic work
so nearly purely Indian in its form.

Sometimes the leaves are much elaborated as in one of

RIPON, *late Fifteenth Century.*

the late misericordes of Westminster Abbey; in a few cases
the original simplicity is quite lost, and we have, as at Ripon,

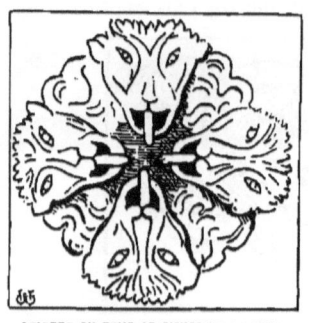

ROSETTE ON TOMB OF BISHOP DE LA WICH,
CHICHESTER.

the mask idea run mad, inverted, and the leaves become
a graceful composition of foliage, flower, and fruit.

A rosette from the tomb
of Bishop de La Wich, Chichester, has four animal faces in
an excellent design.

. Often masks are of the
simple description known as
the Notch-head; these are of
the thirteenth and fourteenth centuries.   They are generally
found in exposed situations at some elevation, as among the
series of corbels (*corbula* a small basket) or brackets called

the corbel-table, supporting a stone course or cornice. The
likeness to the human face caused by the shadows of the T
varies in different examples. That below, by curving back at
the base, suggests the idea of a mouth. Occasionally, as at
Finedon, Northamptonshire, the notch-head has its likeness
to a face increased by the addition of ears.

Norman masks are interesting, as they explain some
odd appearances in later work. In many churches are faces
scored with lines across the cheeks, regardless of the ordinary
lines of expression, in a manner closely resembling the tattoo
incisions of the New Zealand warrior.
This appearance, however, is simply the
too faithful copying of crude Norman
masks, in which the lines are meant
to be the semi-circles round eyes and
mouth. Moreover, the Norman heads
are most often the heads of animals
grinning to shew the teeth, although

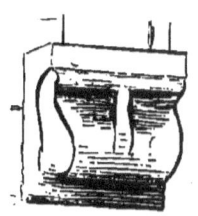

MASK, BUCKLE, OR NOTCH HEAD,
CULHAM, YORKSHIRE.

their general effect is that of grotesque human heads. Iffley
west doorway furnishes the best example. Here we have
the well-known "beak head" ornament. The semicircle and
upper portion of the jambs have single heads, not two of
which are exactly alike, though all closely resemble each
other. They are heads of the eagle or gryphon order, with
a forehead ornament very Assyrian in character. The heads
of the jambs are compound, being the head of a grinning
beast, probably a lion, from the mouth of which emerges a
gryphon head of small size. These are sometimes called

"Cat-heads," and the gryphon head is sometimes considered
(and perhaps occasionally shewn as such) a tongue.   A fine
doorway of beak-heads is at St. Peter's-in-the-East, Oxford,
which church was probably executed by the workmen who
were responsible for Iffley.

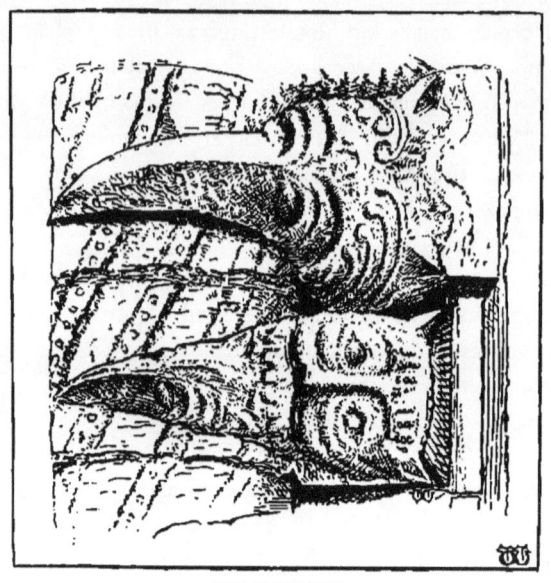

BEAK HEADS, IFFLEY.

It is probable that the symbolism of this is the swallowing
up of night by day or *vice versâ*.   The outer arch of the Iffley
doorway consists of zodiacal signs, and at the south doorway
are other designs elsewhere mentioned in this volume, far
removed from Christian intent.

The grotesqueness of Norman work is almost entirely unconscious. The workers were full of Byzantine ideas, and the severe and awful was their object rather than the comic.

They frequently attempted pretty detail in their symbolic designs, but in all the forms which have come from their chisels it is easy to see how incomplete an embodiment they gave to their conceptions, or rather to the conceptions of their traditional school. Norman work, beyond the Gothic, irrespective of the architectural peculiarities, has traces of its eastern origin in the classic connection of its

NORMAN MASK, ROCHESTER.

designs. Adel Church, near Leeds, is peculiar in having co-mingled with its eastern designs more than ordinarily tangible references to ancient Keltic worship, but nearly all

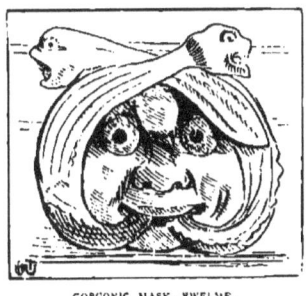

GORGONIC MASK, EWELME.

Norman ideographic detail concerns itself with old-world myths.

An excellent conception, well carried out, is in a mask which is one of a series of late carvings alternating with the gargoyles of Ewelme. In this, instead of leaves issuing from the mouth of the mask, there are two dragons. If those with leaves are deities, this surely must be one of the Furies. It is on the north side of the nave ; on the exterior of the aisle, at the same side, other sculptures form a kind of irregular corbel-table, and special attention may be drawn to them as affording an indication of the derivation of such ornaments

FOLIATE MASK, EWERLME.

from the "antefixes" or decorated tiles occupying a nearly corresponding position in classic architecture.

One of those on the aisle offers a further explanation of the mark before mentioned as being on the foreheads of some masks. In this case the prominences of the eyebrows branch off into foliage. This appears also to be the intention in a capital carving in Lincoln Chapter House.

Roslyn Chapel has some very realistic heads, notably of apes or gorillas near the south doorway, of which one is drawn (opposite).

Norman work has frequently some very grotesque heads in corbel tables and tower corners, to the

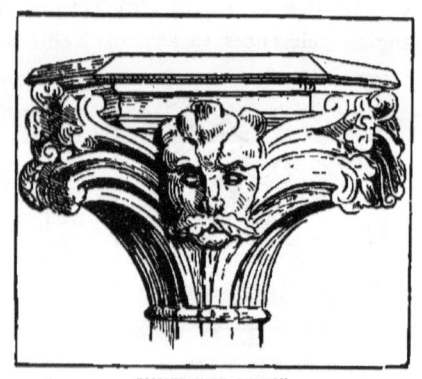

FOLIATE MASK, LINCOLN.

odd appearance of which the decay by weather has no doubt much contributed. Two examples from Sutton

Courtney, Oxfordshire, illustrate this weather-worn whimsicality.

Then comes a crowd of faces which have no particular significance, being simply the outcome of the unrestrainable fun of the carver. Some are merely oddities, while others are full of life-like character.

GORILLA, ROSLYN CHAPEL.

GARGOYLE, SUTTON COURTNEY.

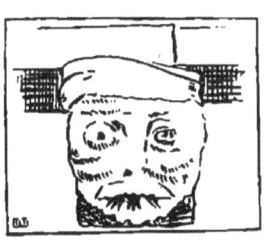

WEATHER-WORN NORMAN, SUTTON
COURTNEY, BERKSHIRE.

The knight with the twisted beard, from Swine, may

HUMOUR, YORK.

MASK WITH SAUSAGE,
STRATFORD-UPON-AVON.

A JEALOUS EYE, YORK.

17

be a portrait, and the Gargantuan-faced dominus from St. Mary's Minster certainly is. An old barbarian head from a

A BEARD WITH A TWIST, SWINE, YORKSHIRE.

A QUIZZICAL VISAGE, BAKEWELL.

croche or elbow-rest at Bakewell is rude and worn, but yet bold and fine.

GRIMACE MAKER, BEVERLEY MINSTER.

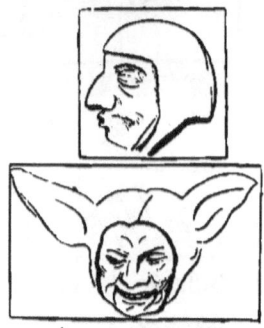

FOOL'S HEADS, BEVERLEY MINSTER.

Some of these are better than the joculators and mimes' faces in which the artist seriously set himself a humorous

A PORTRAIT, ST. MARY'S MINSTER, ISLE OF THANET.

A ROUGH CHARACTER, BAKEWELL.

task, as in the three heads (page 130) from Beverley Minster, though the latter are in some respects more grotesque.

Another curious instance of a grimace and posture maker, assisting his counten-ance's contortions by the use of his fingers, is at Dorchester Abbey. In this the artist has not been master of the facial anatomy, and shows a double pair of lips, one pair in repose, the other pulled back at the corners.

GRIMACE MAKER, DORCHESTER, OXON.

Often a grotesque face will be found added to a beautiful design of foliage, either as the conventional mask, as in the design in Lincoln Chapter House, or a realistic head, as the following grim, dour visage between graceful curves on a misericord at King's College, Cambridge.

GRACE AND THE GRACELESS, KINGS COLLEGE, CAMBRIDGE.

The Domestic and Popular.

THE WEAKER VESSEL, SHERBORNE.

DOMESTIC and popular incidents are plentiful among the carvings, of which they form, indeed, a distinct class; and they afford a considerable amount of material with which might be built up, in a truly Hogarthian and exaggerated spirit, an elaborate account of mediæval manners in general. In the majority of cases the incidents have a familiar, if not an endearing suggestiveness.

DOMESTIC DISCIPLINE, BEVERLEY MINSTER.

The records of mankind are not wanting in stormy incidents in which the gentle female spirit has chafed under some presumed foolishness or wickedness of the head of the house, and at length breaking bounds, inflicted on him personal reminders that patience endureth but for a season. An example of this is given above, which shews the possibility of such a thing as far back as 1520, the date of the Beverley Minster misericordes. While the lady is devoting her

AN UNKIND FARE, BEVERLEY MINSTER.

attention to the flagellation of her unfortunate and perhaps entirely blameless spouse, a dog avails himself of the opportunity to rifle the caldron.

The picture in the initial, taken from a carving in the choir of Sherborne Minster, shews another domestic incident in which the lady administers castigation. Though in itself no more than a vulgar satire, it is probable that this carving was copied from some representation of St. Lucy, who is sometimes shewn with a staff in her hand, and behind her the devil prostrate.

It is not easy to say what is the meaning of another carving in Beverley Minster, or whether it has any connection with that just noted. The probability is that it has not. This may be a shrewish wife being wheeled in the tumbril to the waterside, there to undergo for the better ruling of her tongue, a punishment the authority for which was custom older than law. But I am inclined to think that another reading will be nearer the truth. The vehicle is not the tumbril but a wheelbarrow, and the man propelling it is younger than the lady, who is pulling his hair. I imagine the man is apprentice or husband, and is not very cheerfully trundling his companion home. A similar, but more definite misericorde is in Ripon Cathedral.

In this barrow, the old woman, wearing a cap with hat on the top, as yet occasionally seen in country places, is seated in a mistress-like way. She is not committing any violence, but apparently is offering the man (call him the bridegroom) his choice of either a bag of money with dutiful obedience, or a huge cudgel, which she wields with muscular power, with dereliction. The gem of the carving is the man's face. He smiles a quiet, amused, satirical smile, as of one who would say, "'Tis no harm to humour these foolish old bodies, and must be done, I trow."

But the object called a bag of money is as likely to be a bottle, and the whole subject may be something quite different. She may be going to the doctor, or offering the

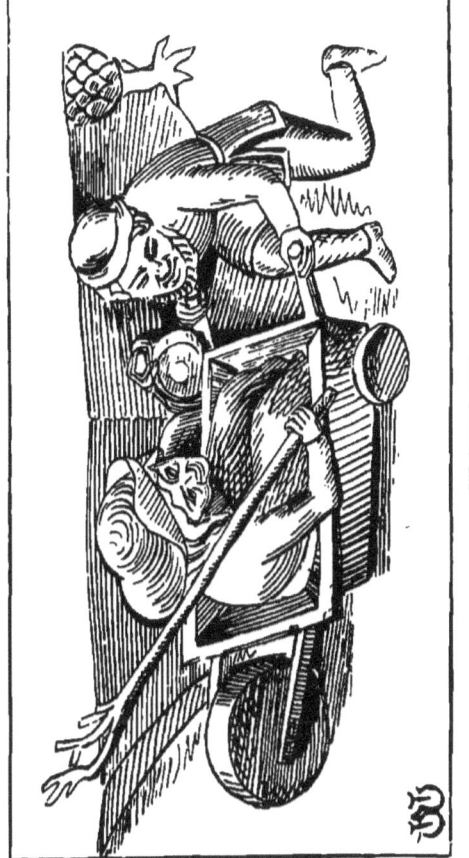

THE CHARIOT, RIPON.

man a drink ; or it may be Noah wheeling his wife into the Ark, which, it was one of the jokes in a Mystery play to suppose she was very unwilling to enter.

PILGRIMAGE IN COMFORT, CANTERBURY.

The block from the capital of a column in the crypt of Canterbury Cathedral, tells us little of its history.   It is given

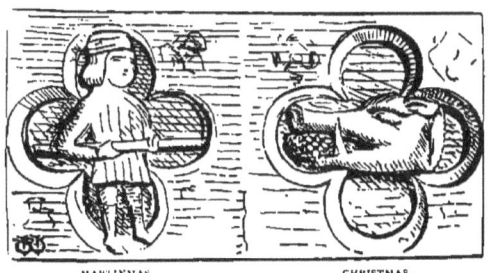

MARTINMAS.   CHRISTMAS.

HOLY TRINITY, HULL.

as an example of a cheerful grace and ease not common in
early work.

The hunting of the boar is a frequent subject of the
Gothic carver, being generally considered the sport of
September, though Sir Edward Coke says the season for the
boar was from Christmas to Candlemas. It is uncommon to
find the boar's head shewn treated as in the accompanying
block, struck off, and with the lemon in his mouth, ready for

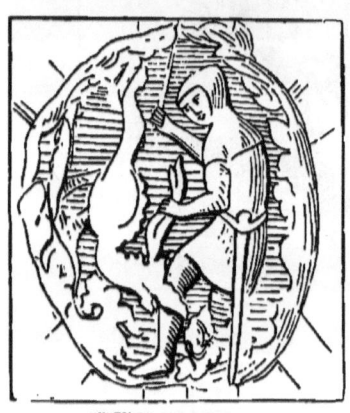

the table. These quatre-
foils are the only two
with a special design upon
them, out of twelve on
the font of Holy Trinity
Church, Hull, the others
having rosettes. There
is no rule in this, but
there are other examples
in which small portions
of fonts are picked out
for significant decoration,
and possibly on the side

HUNTSMAN AND DEER, YORK.

originally intended to be turned towards the door of the
church, or the altar.

Hunting scenes frequently occur. A boss in York
Minster shews a huntsman "breaking" a deer as it hangs
from a tree.

The wild sweetness of one stringed and one wind
instrument—not uncommonly met as harp and piccolo near

London "saloon bars"—was a usual duet of the middle ages. In Stoeffler's *Calendarum Romanorum Magnum* (of 1518) in a series of woodcuts illustrating the months, and which are otherwise reasonable, he gives one of these duets performed in a field as a proper occupation of the month of April with the following highly appropriate distich—

"Aprilis patule nucis sub umbra
    post convivia dormio libenter.'

A CURIOUS DUET, CHICHESTER.

In this carving, however, the musicians appear to be within doors and to be giving a set duet. To the interest of the ear they add a curious spectacle for the eye, for they are seated in chairs which have no fore-legs, and their balance is kept by the flageoletist taking hold of the harp as the players sit facing, so that while leaning back they form a counter-poise to each other. The chairs are a curious study in mediæval furniture.

It is not unlikely that the sculptor in the case of the

annexed block had in his mind something similar to the
saying—

"When a man's single he lives at his ease."

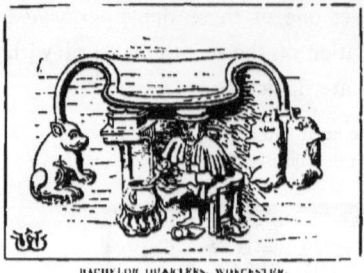

BACHELOR QUARTERS, WORCESTER.

A man come in from,
we may presume, frost and
snow, has taken off his
boots, and warms his feet
as, seated on his fald-stool
by the fire, he stirs the
pot with lively anticipation
of the meal preparing in-
side.   He is probably a shepherd or swine-herd ; on one side
is seated his dog, at the other are hung two fat gammons
of bacon.

Shepherds and shepherding furnish frequent subjects to
the carver.

In a Coventry Corpus Christi play of 1534 one of the

three shepherds presents his gloves to the infant Saviour in these words—

> " Have here my myttens, to pytt en thi hondis,
> Other treysure have I none to present thee with."

This carving has been called the Good Shepherd. If the artist really meant Christ by this shepherd with a hood over his head and hat over that, with great gloves and shoes, with a round beardless face, with his arms round the necks of two sheep, holding their feet in his hands, it is the finest piece of religious burlesque extant. But it is not to be supposed that the idea even occurred to the sculptor.

The Feast of Fools was a kind of religious farce, a "mystery" run riot. Cedranus, a Byzantine historian, who wrote in the eleventh century, records that it was introduced into the Greek Church A.D. 990, by Theophylact, patriarch of Constantinople. We can partly understand that the popular craving for the wild liberties of the Saturnalia might be met, and perhaps modified, by a brief removal of the solemn constraint of the Christian priest-rule. But licentiousness in church worship was no new thing, and, long before the time of Theophylact, the Church of the West, and probably the Greek Church also, had been rendered scandalous by the laxity with which the church services were conducted. At the Council of Orleans, in A.D. 533, it was found necessary to rule that no person in a church shall sing, drink, or do anything unbecoming ; at another in Châlons, in A.D. 650, women were forbidden to sing indecent songs in church.

There is in fact every evidence, including the sculptures of our subject, that religion was not, popularly, a thing solemn in itself. Cedranus mentions the "diabolic dances" among the enormities practised at the Feast of Fools, which was generally held about Christmas, though not confined to that festival.

In the twelfth century, the abuse increased; songs of the most indecent and offensive character were sung in the midst

DANCING FOOLS, BEVERLEY MINSTER.

of the mock services; puddings were eaten, and dice rattled on the altar, and old shoes burnt as incense.

This observance, so evidently an expedient parody of the old-time festivals, is traceable in England, and said to have been abolished about the end of the fourteenth century. The carvings in Beverley Minster, here presented, are supposed to refer to the Feast, and at any rate give us a good idea of the mediæval fool. There were innumerable classic

19

dances.   The Greeks send down the names of two hundred
kinds.   A dance with arms was the Pyrrhic dance, which was
similar in some of its varieties to the military dance known as
the Morris.   The Morris was introduced into Spain by the
Moors, and brought into England by John of Gaunt in 1332.
It was, however, little used until the reign of Henry VII.
There were other vivacious dances, called Bayle, of Moorish
origin, which, as well as various kinds of the stately Court
dance, were used by the Spaniards.   It is difficult, from
general sources, to ascertain the dances in vogue in old
England.   A drawing in the Cotton MSS. shews a Saxon
dancing a reel.   The general inference is, however, that the
Morris (of the Moors or Moriscoes) was the chief dance of the
English, and perhaps it is that in which the saltatory fools of
the carving are engaged.

Probably the extraordinary monstrosity shewn in the
annexed block had an actual existence.   There are fairly
numerous accounts of such malformities in mediæval times,
and it was a function of mediæval humour to make capital out
of unfortunate deformity.   This poor man has distorted hands
instead of feet, and he moves about on pattens or wooden
clogs strapped to his hands and legs.   There is little meaning
in the side carvings.   The fool-ape, making an uncouth
gesture, is perhaps to shew the character of those who mock
misfortune.   The man with the scimitar may represent the
alarm of one who might suddenly come upon the sight of the
abortion, and fearing some mystery or trap, draw his blade.
In a sense this is a humourous carving—·yet there is a quality

for which it is much more remarkable, and that is its element of forcible and realistic pathos.

Two reliefs from York Minster are presumably scenes

from classic mythology, from, in regard to the costumes, a Saxon point of view. One may be supposed to be the rape of Ganymede. Oak leaves are an attribute of Jupiter, as is also the eagle which bore Ganymede to Olympus.

The other may be Vulcan giving Venus "a piece of his mind."

A MYTHOLOGICAL EPISODE, YORK.

If these readings are correct these two carvings are among the very few instances of representations of circumstantial detail of the Olympian mythology.   Most of the church references to mythology have more connection with the earlier symbolic meanings than with the later narrative histories into which the cults degenerated.   Other examples are in the references

MARITAL VIOLENCE, YORK.

to Hercules in the sixteenth century stalls of Henry VII.'s Chapel, Westminster.

There is in mediæval art several examples remaining of what may be called topsy-turveyism, in which two figures mutually lent their parts to each other in such a way that four figures may be found.

An excellent example of this is at New College, Oxford, in which, though the four figures are so apparent when once

A CONTINUOUS GROUP OF FOUR FIGURES, OXFORD.

seen, the two (taken as upper and lower), are in a natural and ingenious acrobatic position. The grotesque head at the base is put in to balance the composition, and perhaps to prevent the trick being discerned at once.

The grace of the free if somewhat meagre Corinthian acanthus as used in Early English work is often rendered more marked by the introduction of an extraneous subject. Thus at Wells the foliate design is relieved by the ungainly figure of a melancholy individual, who, before retiring to rest, pursues an examination into his pedal callosities, or extracts the poignant thorn.   Or can it be that we have here a reminder of the Egyptian monarch, Sómarája, mentioned in

A PILGRIM'S PAINS, WELLS.

the Hindoo accounts of the Egyptian mythology, who was dissolute and outcast, and who, to shew his repentance and patience, stood twelve days upon one leg?

This discursive chapter would not be complete without a reference to the alleged impropriety of church grotesques. Though it is not to be denied that in the wide range of subjects a considerable number of indecent subjects have crept in, yet their proportion is small.   Examination would lead to the belief that upon the whole the art of the churches is much purer than the literature or the popular taste of the respective periods.   Though there may be sometimes met examples of grossness of humour and a frank want of reserve, such as in the annexed drawing from the chapel of All Souls,

Oxford, yet these are rarely of the most gross or least reserved character.

It may be well to note, in this connection that the literature from which we draw the bulk of our ideas as to

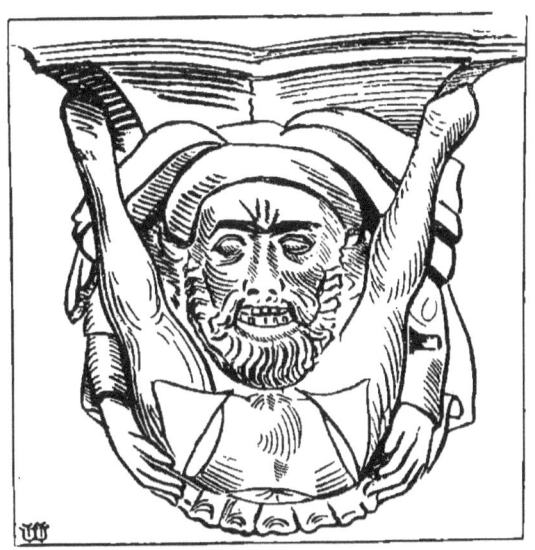

A POSTURIST, ALL SOUL'S, OXFORD.

mediæval life, are foreign, and that, although English manners would not be remotely different in essentials, yet there would be as many absolute differences as there are yet remaining to our eyes in architecture and in art generally.

The Pig and other Animal Musicians.

APE AS PIPER, BEVERLEY

NE might count in the churches animal musicians, perhaps, by thousands, and the reason of their presence is doubtless the same as that which explains the frequency of the serious carvings of musicians which adorn the arches of nave and choir through-out the country — namely the prevalent use of various kinds of instrumental music in the service of the church. The animal musicians are the burlesques of the human, and the fact that the pig is the most frequent performer may perhaps suggest that the ability of the musician had overwhelmed the consideration of other qualities which might be expected, but were not found, in the harmony-producing choristers. Clever as musicians, they may have become merely functionaries as regards interest in the church, as we see to-day in the case of our bell-ringers, who for the most part issue from the churches as worshippers enter them.

It may also be that the frequency of suilline musicians may have derisive reference to the ancient veneration in which the pig was held in the mythologies. It was a symbol of the sun, and, derivatively, of fecundity. Perhaps the strongest trace of this is in Scandinavian mythology. The northern races sacrificed a boar to Freyr, the patron deity of Sweden and of Iceland, the god of fertility : he was fabled to ride upon a boar named Gullinbrusti, or Golden Bristle. Freyr's festival was at Yule-tide. Yule is *jul* or *heol*, the sun, and Gehul is the Saxon "Sunfeast." The gods of Scandinavia were said to nightly feast upon the great boar Sæhrimnir, which eaten up, was every morning found whole again. This

seems somewhat akin to the Hindoo story of Crórásura, a demon with the face of a boar, who continually read the Vedas and was so devout that Vishnu (the sun god) gave him a boon. He asked that no creature existing in the three worlds might have power to slay him, which was granted.

SOW AND FIDDLE, WINCHESTER.

The special sacrifice of the pig was not peculiar to Scandinavia, for the Druids and the Greeks also offered up a boar at the winter solstice. The sacrifice of a pig was a constant preliminary of the Athenian assemblies. As a corn destroyer the same animal was sacrificed to Ceres.

The above explains the recurrence of the pig rather than the pig musician. A pregnant sow was, however, yearly sacrificed to Mercury, the inventor of the harp, and a sow playing the harp is among the rich set of choir carvings in Beverley Minster.

20

The chase of the boar was the sport of September, the ordinary killing season, the swine being then in condition after

SOW AS HARPIST, BEVERLEY MINSTER.

their autumn feed of *bucon*, or beechmast (hence *bacon*), "His Martinmas has come" passed into a proverb. The prevalence of the pig as a food animal had undoubtedly its share in the frequency of art reference.

In the Christian adoption of pagan attributes, the pig was apportioned to St. Anthony, it is said, variously, because he had been a swineherd, or lived in woods. The smallest or weakling pig in a litter, called in the north "piggy-widdy" (small white pig), and in the south midlands the "dillin" (perhaps equivalent to *delayed*), and is elsewhere styled the Anthony pig, as specially needing the protection of his patron.

A common representation of the pig musician is a

MUSIC AT DINNER, WINCHESTER.

sow who plays to her brood. At Winchester, the feast of the little ones is enlivened by the strains of the double flute. At

Durham Castle, in a carving formerly in Aucland Castle Chapel, the sow plays the bagpipes while the young pigs dance. At Ripon, a vigorous carving has the same subject, and another at Beverley, in which a realistic trough forms the foreground.

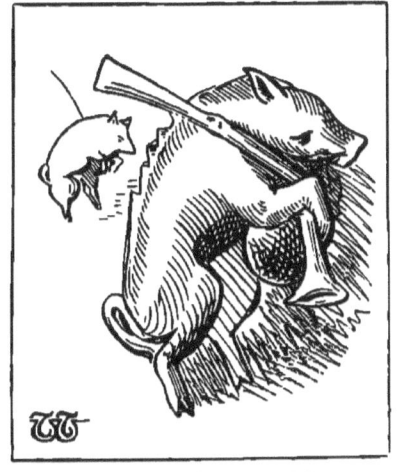

The "Pig and Whistle" forms an old tavern sign. Dr. Brewer explains this as the pot, bowl, or cup (the *pig*), and the wassail it contained. The earthenware vessel used to warm the feet

SOW AND BAGPIPES, DURHAM CASTLE

in bed is in Scotland yet called "the pig," and to southern

PIGS AND PIPES, RIPON.

strangers the use of the word has caused a temporary embarrassment. If this explanation is not coincident with some other not at present to hand, the carving of the

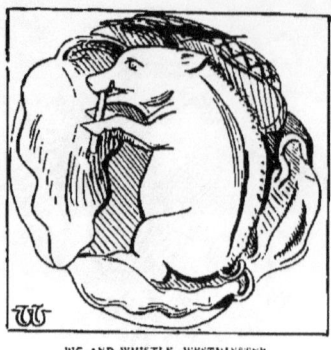

pig and whistle in the sixteenth century carving in Henry VII.'s chapel shows that the corruption of the " pig and wassail " was accepted in ignorance as far back as that period.

But too much stress is not to be laid upon the pig as a musician, for at Westminster the bear plays the

PIG AND WHISTLE, WESTMINSTER.

bagpipes, just as at Winchester the ape performs on the harp. In the Beverley Minster choir an ape converts a cat into an almost automatic instrument by biting its tail.

APE AS HARPIST, WESTMINSTER.

Compound Forms.

N nearly every church compound forms are met which in a high degree merit the designation of grotesque. Few religions have been without these symbolic representations of complex characters. If the Egyptian had its cat-headed and hawk-headed men, the Assyrian its human-headed bull, the Mexican its serpent-armed tiger-men, so also the Scandinavian mythology had its horse-headed and vulture-headed giants, and its human-headed eagle. Horace, who doubtless knew the figurative meaning of what he satirizes, viewed the representations of such compounds in his days, and asks—

> "If in a picture you should see
> A handsome woman with a fishes tail,
> Or a man's head upon a horse's neck,
> Or limbs of beasts of the most diff'rent kind,
> Cover'd with feathers of all sorts of birds
> Would you not laugh?"*

It is, perhaps, a little remote from our subject to inquire whether the poet or the priest came the first in bringing about these archaic combinations; yet a word or two may be devoted to suggesting the inquiry. It is probable that the religious ideas and artistic forms met in ancient worships first solely

* Roscommon.

existed in poetic expressions of the qualities of the sun—of the other members of the solar system—of the gods. Thus the swiftness of the sun in his course and in his light induced the mention of wings. Hence the wings of an eagle added to a circular form arose as the symbol in one place; in another arose the God Mercury ; while Jove the great sun-god is shewn accompanied by an eagle. The fertility of the earth became as to corn Ceres, as to vines Bacchus, as to flowers Flora, and so forth. The human personification, in cases where a combination of qualities or functions was sought to be indicated, resulted in more or less abstruse literary fables; on the other hand the artist or symbol seeker found it easier to select a lower plane of thought for his embodiments. Thus, while swiftness suggested the eagle, strength was figured by the lion : so when a symbol of swiftness and strength was required arose the compound eagle-lion, the gryphon.

The gryphon, however, though constantly met in Gothic, is rarely grotesque in itself. Another form which also, to a certain extent, is incorruptible, is that of the sphinx. This is a figure symbolic of the sun from the Egyptian point of view, in which the Nile was all-important. Nilus, or Ammon, the Egyptian Jove, was the sun-god, an equivalent to Osiris, and the sphinx was similar in estimation, being, it is reasonably conjectured, a compound of Leo and Virgo, at whose conjunction the Nile has yearly risen. According to Dr. Birch, the sphinx is to be read as being the symbol of Harmachis or "the sun on the horizon." It may be that the

Child rising from the Shell is sunrise over the sea, and the Sphinx sunrise over the land. It has been conjectured that

the cherubim of the taber-
nacle were sphinx-form.
The cherubim on the
Mosaic Ark are among
the subjects of the earliest
mention of composite
symbols. Ezekiel says
they were composed of
parts of the figures of a

SPHINX AND BUCKLER, BEVERLEY MINSTER.

man (wisdom, intellect), a lion (dominion), a bull (strength), and an eagle (sharp-sightedness, swiftness.) The Persians and Hindoos had similar figures. A man with buffalo horns

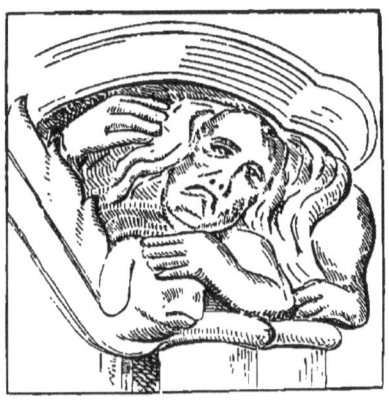

SPHINX FIGURE, DORCHESTER, OXON.

is painted in the Syn-
hedria of the American
Indians in conjunction
with that of a panther
or puma-like beast,
and these are supposed
to be a contraction of
the cherubimical fig-
ures of the man, the
bull, and the lion ;
these, renewed yearly,
are near the carved

figures of eagles common in the Indian sun-worship.

A carving in the arm-rest of one of the stalls of Beverley

Minster, suggested in the block on page 159, shews a sphinx
with a shield; there are in the same church several fine
examples seated in the orthodox manner.

On a capital in the sedilia of Dorchester Abbey is a
curious compound which may be classed as a sphinx. One
of the hands (or paws) is held over the eyes of a dog, which
suggests the manner in which animals were anciently sacrificed.
Another sphinx in the same sedilia is of the winged variety.

COWLED SPHINX, DORCHESTER, OXON.

It has the head cowled; many of
the mediæval combinatory forms
are mantled.

In Worcester Cathedral is a
compound of man, ox, and lion,
very different from the sphinx or
cherubim shapes, being a grotesque
deprived of all the original poetry
of the conception.

Virgil describes Scylla (the
Punic *Scol,* destruction) as a
beautiful figure upwards, half her body being a beautiful
virgin; downwards, a horrible fish with a wolf's belly (utero).
Homer similarly.

The mermaid is a frequent subject, but more monotonous
in its form and action than any other creature, and is generally
found executed with a respectful simplicity that scarcely ever
savours of grotesqueness. The mermaid, "the sea wolf of the
abyss," and the "mighty sea-woman" of Boewulf, has an
early origin as a deity of fascinating but malignant tendencies.

The centaur, perhaps, ranks next to the sphinx in artistic merit. To the early Christians the centaur was merely a symbol of unbridled passions, and all mediæval reference classes it as evil. Virgil mentions it as being met in numbers near the gates of Hades, and the Parthenon sculptures shew it as the enemy of men.

GROTESQUE CHERUBIM, WORCESTER.

The story of the encyclopedias regarding centaurs is that they were Thessalonian horsemen, whom the Greeks, ignorant of horsemanship, took to be half-men, half-animals. They were called, it is said, centaurs, from their skill in killing the wild bulls of the Pelion mountains, and, later, hippo-centaurs.

21

This explanation may, in the presence of other combinatory forms, be considered doubtful, as it is more probable that this, like those, arose out of a poetic appreciation of the qualities underlying beauty of form, that is, out of an intelligent symbolism. The horse, where known, was always a favourite animal among men. Innumerable coinages attest this fact. Early Corinthian coins have the figure of Pegasus. In most the horse is shewn alone. In the next proportion he is attached to a chariot. In few is he shewn being ridden, as it is his qualities that were intended to be expressed, and not those of the being who has subjected him. One of the old Greek gold staters has a man driving a chariot in which the horse has a human head; while the man is urging the horse with the sacred three-branched rod, each branch of which terminates in a trefoil. The centaur has a yet unallotted place in the symbolism of the sun-myth. Classic mythology says Chiron the centaur was the teacher of Apollo in music, medicine, and hunting, and centaurs are mostly sagittarii or archers, whose arrows, like those of Apollo, are the sunbeams. The centaur met in Gothic ornament is the Zodiacal Sagittarius, and true to this original derivation, the centaur is generally found with his bow and arrow.

It is said that the Irish saints, Ciaran and Nessan, are the same with the centaurs Chiron and Nessus.

A capital of the south doorway, Iffley, has a unique composition of centaurs. A female centaur, armed with bow (broken) and arrow, is suckling a child centaur after the human manner. The equine portions of the figures are in

MATERNAL CARES OF THE CENTAUR. IFFLEY.

exceptionally good drawing, though the tremendous elongation of the human trunks, and the ill-rendered position, render the group very grotesque. Both the mother and child wear the classic cestus or girdle. The bow carried by the mother is held apparently in readiness in the left hand, while it is probable that the right breast was meant to be shown removed, as was stated of the Amazons. The mother looks

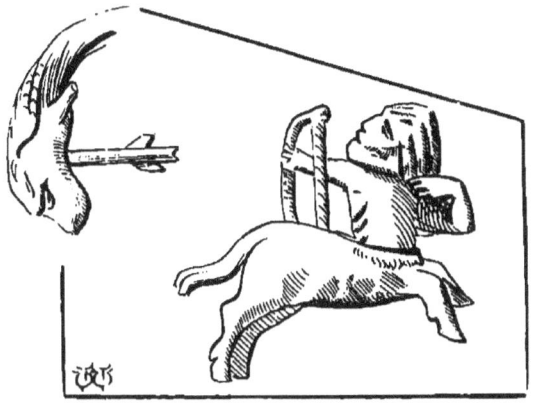

CENTAUR AS DRAGON SLAYER, EXETER.

off, and there is an air of alertness about the two, which is explained by the sculpture on the return of the capital, where the father-centaur is seen slaying a wolf, lion, or other beast.

On a centaur at Exeter of the thirteenth century, the mythical idea is somewhat retained ; the centaur has shot an arrow into the throat of a dragon, which is part of the ornament. This is a very rude but suggestive carving. Is the centaur but a symbol of Apollo himself?

The next block (at Ely) is also of the centaur order, though not suggestive of aggression. The figure is female, and

MUSICAL CENTAUR, ELY.

she is playing the zither. This is of the fourteenth century.

Another classic conception which has been perpetuated

HARPY. WINCHESTER.

in Gothic is the harpy, though in most cases without any apparent recognition of the harpy character. Exceptions are such instances as that of the harpy drawn in the chapter "Satires without Satan." In one at Winchester a fine mediæval effect is produced by putting a hood on the human head.

Another curious bird combination is in a carving in the Architectural Museum, Tufton Street, London, from an un-known church. This is a semi-human figure, whose upper part is skilfully draped. The head, bent towards the ground, is that of a bird of the ibis species, and it is probable that we have here a relic of the Egyptian Mercury Thoth, who was incarnated as an ibis. Thoth is called the God of the Heart (the conscience), and the ibis was said to be sacred to him

IBIS-HEADED FIGURE FROM AN UNKNOWN CHURCH.

because when sleeping it assumes the shape of a heart.

An unusual compound is that of a swan with the agreeable head of a young woman, in St. George's Chapel, Windsor. This may be one of the swan-sisters in the old story of the " Knight of the Swan."

THE SWAN SISTER, ST. GEORGE'S CHAPEL, WINDSOR.

The initial letter of this section is a fine grotesque rendering of the Egyptian goddess Athor, Athyr, or Het-her (meaning the dwell-ing of God.) She was the daughter of the sun, and bore in images the sun's disc. Probably through a lapse into ignorance on the part of the priest-painters, she became of less consideration, and the signification even of her image was forgotten. She had always had as one of her representations, a bird with a human head horned and bearing the disc ; but the disc began to be shewn as a tambourine, and she herself was styled "the mistress of dance and jest." As in the cosmogony of one of the Egyptian Trinities she was the Third Person, as Supreme Love, the Greeks held her to be the same as Aphrodite. The name of the sun-disc was Aten, and its worship was kindred to that of Ra, the mid-day sun. The Hebrew Adonai and the Syriac Adonis have been considered to be derived from this word Aten.

Several examples of bird-compounds are in the Exeter series of misericordes of the thirteenth century. They are renderings in wood of the older Anglo-Saxon style of design, and are ludicrously grotesque.

It is scarcely to be considered that the compound figures were influenced by the prevalence of mumming in the periods of the various carvings. In this, as in many other respects, the traditions of the carvers' art protected it from being coloured by the aspect of the times, except in a limited degree, shewn in distinctly isolated examples.

BIRD-COMPOUND, EXETER.

Non-descripts.

A BEARDED BIPED, ST. KATHERINE'S.

HERE is a large number of bizarre works which defy natural classification, and though in many cases they are a branch of the compound order of figures, yet they are frequently well defined as non-descripts. These, though in one respect the most grotesque of the grotesques, do not claim lengthy description. Where they are not traceable compounds, they are often apparently the creatures of fancy, without meaning and without history. It may be, however, that could we trace it, we should find for each a pedigree as interesting, if not as old, as that of any of the sun-myths. Among the absurd figures which scarcely call for explanation are such as that shown in the initial, from the Hospital and Collegiate Church of St. Katherine by the Tower (now removed to a substituted hospital in Regent's Park).

A CLOAKED SIN, TUFTON STREET.

In the Architectural Museum, Tufton Street, London,

22

is a carving from an unknown church, in which appear two figures which were not an uncommon subject for artists of the odd.   These are human heads, to which are attached legs without intermediary bodies, and with tails depending from the back of the heads.

In the " Pilgremage of the Sowle," printed by Caxton in 1483, translated from a French manuscript of 1435 or earlier, is a description of a man's conscience, which, there is little doubt, furnished the idealic material for these carvings.   A

THE WORM OF CONSCIENCE.
(From an unknown Church.)

"sowle" being "snarlyed in the trappe" of Satan, is being, by a travesty on the forms of a court of law, claimed by both the "horrible Sathanas" and its own Warden or Guardian Angel. The Devil calls for his chief witness by the name of Synderesys, but the witness calls himself the Worm of Conscience.   The following is the soul's description :—"Then came forth by me an old one, that long time had hid himself nigh me, which before that time I had not perceived.   He was wonderfully hideous and of cruel countenance ; and he began to grin, and shewed me his jaws and gums, for teeth he had none, they all being broken and worn away. He had no body, but under his head he had only a tail, which seemed the tail of a worm of exceeding length and greatness." This strange accuser tells the Soul that he had often warned it, and so often bitten it that all his teeth were wasted and broken, his function being "to bite and wounde them that wrong themselves."*

The above examples are scarcely unique. In Ripon Cathedral, on a misericorde of 1489, representing the bearing

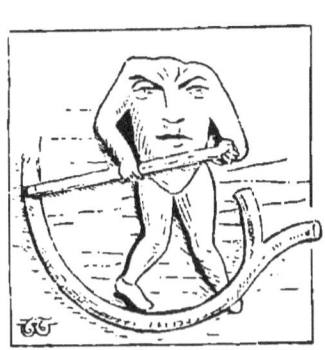

NOBODIES, RIPON.

of the grapes of Eschol on a staff, are two somewhat similar figures, likewise mere "nobodies," though without tails. These are a covert allusion to the wonderful stories of the spies, which, it is thus hinted, are akin to the travellers' tales of mediæval times, as well as a pun on the report that they had seen nobody.

It is evident that the idea of men without bodies came

* Hone.

from the East, and also that it had credence as an actual fact. In the *Cosmographiæ Universalis*, printed in 1550, they are alluded to in the following terms :—" Sunt qui cervicibus carent et in humeris habet oculos ; De India ultra Gangem fluvium sita."

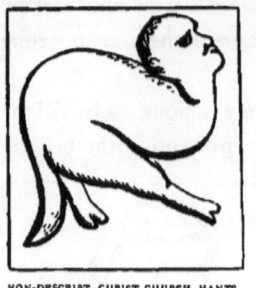

There are many carvings which are more or less of the same character, and probably intended to embody the idea of conscience or sins.

The two rather indecorous figures shewn in the following block from Great Malvern are varieties doubtless typifying sins.

NON-DESCRIPT, CHRIST CHURCH, HANTS.

SINS IN SYMBOL, GREAT MALVERN.

Rebuses.

ROLT-TON.

REBUSES are often met among Gothic sculptures, but not in such frequency, or with an amount of humour to claim any great attention here. They are almost entirely, as in the case of the canting heraldry of seals, of late date, being mostly of the 15th and 16th centuries. They are often met as the punning memorial of the name of a founder, builder, or architect, as the bolt-ton of Bishop Bolton in St. Bartholomew's, Smithfield, the many-times-repeated cock of Bishop Alcock in Henry VII's. Chapel, the eye and the slip of a tree, and the man slipping from a tree, for Bishop Islip, Westminster; and others well known. In the series of misericordes in Beverley Minster, there are *arma palantes* of the dignitaries of the Church in 1520. William White, the Chancellor, has no less than seven different renderings of the pun upon his

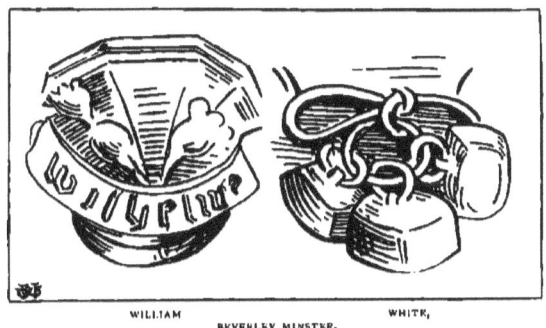

WILLIAM   WHITE,

BEVERLEY MINSTER.

name, all being representations of weights, apparently of four-stone ponderosity.   Thomas Donnington, the Precentor, whose name would doubtless often be written Do'ington, has

WEIGHT, REBUS FOR WHITE, BEVERLEY
MINSTER.

a doe upon a ton or barrel. John Sperke, the Clerk of the Fabric, has a dog with a bone, and a vigilant cock ; this, how-ever, is not a name-rebus so much as an allusion to the exigencies of his office.   The Church of St. Nicholas, Lynn, had miseri-cordes (some of which are now in the Architectural Museum) which have several monograms and rebuses.   Unfortunately, they are somewhat involved, and there is at present no key by which to read them.   The least doubtful is that given below.

It has a "ton" rebus which will admit, however, of perhaps three different renderings.   It is most likely Thorn-ton, less so Bar-ton, and still less Hop-ton, all Lincolnshire names.

MERCHANT MARK, COGNIZANCE AND REBUS, ST. NICHOLAS'S, LYNN.

Trinities.

LARVA-LIKE DRAGON, ST. PAUL'S, BEDFORD.

EPEATEDLY has the statement been made that the various mythologies are only so many corruptions of the Mosaic system. Manifestly if this could be admitted there would be little interest in enquiring further into their details. But there are three arguments against the statement, any one of which is effective. Although it is perhaps totally unnecessary to contradict that which can be accepted by the unreflective only, it is sufficiently near the purpose of this volume to slightly touch upon the matter, as pointing strong distinctions among ancient worships.

First, there is the simple fact recorded in the Mosaic account itself, that there existed at that time, and had done previously, various religious systems, the rooting out of which was an important function of the liberated Hebrews. The only reply to this is that, by a slight shift of ground, the mythologies were corruptions of the patriarchal religion, not the Mosaic system. Yet paganism surrounded the patriarchs.

The second point is that most of the mythologies had crystallized into taking the sun as the main symbol of worship, and into taking the equinoxes and other points of the constellation path as other symbols and reminders of periodic worship; whereas in the Mosaic system the whole structure of the solar year is ignored, all the calculations being lunar. If it be objected that Numbers ix. 6-13, and II. Chronicles xxx. 2, refer indirectly to an intercalary month, that, if admitted, could only for expediency's sake, and has no bearing upon the general silence as to the solar periods. This second point is an important testimony to what may be termed Mosaic originality.

The third point is that in most of the mythologies there is the distinct mention of a Trinity; in the Mosaic system, the system of the Old Testament, none. With the question as to whether the New Testament supports the notion of a Trinity, we need not concern ourselves here; it is enough that it has been adopted as an item of the Christian belief.

The mythological Trinities are vague and, of course, difficult or impossible to understand. Most of them appear to be attempts of great minds of archaic times to reconcile the manifest contradictions ever observable in the universe. This is done in various ways. Some omit one consideration, some another; but they generally agree that to have a three-fold character in one deity is necessary in explaining the phenomenon of existence. Some of the Trinities may be recited.

PERSIAN.

OROMASDES, Goodness, the deviser of Creation.

MITHRAS, Eternal Intellect, the architect and ruler of the world, literally " the Friend."

ARIMANES, the mundane soul (Psyche).

GRECIAN.	ROMAN.
ZEUS.	JUPITER, Power.
PALLAS.	MINERVA, Wisdom, Eternal
HERA.	Intellect.
	JUNO, Love.

SCANDINAVIAN.

ODIN, Giver of Life.
HÆNIR, Giver of motion and sense.
LODUR, Giver of speech and the senses.

AMERICAN INDIAN.

OTKON.   MESSOU.   ATAHUATA.

EGYPTIAN.

CNEPH, the Creator, Goodness.
PTA (Opas), the active principle of Creation (= Vulcan).
EICTON.

The Egyptians had other Trinities than the above, each chief city having its own form; in these, however, the third personality appears to be supposed to proceed from the other two, which scarcely seems to have been intended in the instances already given. Some of the city Trinities were as follow :—

THEBES.	PHILAE & ABYDOS.	ABOO-SIMBEL.
AMUN-RA (= Jupiter),	OSIRIS (= Pluto).	PTA or PHTHAH.
(RA = the Mid-day Sun.	ISIS (= Proserpine).	AMUM-RA.
MANT or MENTU (= "the	HORUS, the Saviour,	ATHOR, Love (the
mother," Juno.)	the Shepherd (the	wife of Horus).
CHONSO (= Hercules.)	the Rising Sun).	

So that it is no coincidence that both Hercules and Horus are met in Gothic carvings as deliverers from dragons.

23

ELEPHANTINE.	MEMPHIS.	HELIOPOLIS.
KHUM or CHNOUMIS.	PTAH.	TUM (Setting Sun.)
ANUKA.	MERENPHTAH.	NEBHETP.
HAK.	NEFER-ATUM.	HORUS.

Another Egyptian triad, styled "Trimorphous God!"

was :—	BAIT.	ATHOR.	AKORI.

Another :—TELEPHORUS.   ESCULAPIUS.   SALUS.

VEDIC HINDOO.

AGNI, Fire, governing the Earth.
INDRA, The Firmament, governing Space or Mid Air.
SURYA, The Sun, governing the Heavens.

BRAHMINIC HINDOO.

BRAHMA, the Creator.
VISHNU, the Preserver.
SIVA, the Destroyer (the Transformer) (= Fire).

The Platonic and other philosophic Trinities need not detain us; it has been asserted that by their means the doctrine of the pagan Trinity was grafted on to Christianity.

Right down through the ages the number three has always been regarded as of mystic force. Wherever perfection or efficiency was sought its means were tripled; thus Jove's thunderbolt had three forks of lightning, Neptune's lance was a trident, and Pluto's dog had three heads. The Graces, the Fates, and the Furies were each three. The trefoil was held sacred by the Greeks as well as other triad forms. In the East three was almost equally regarded. Three stars are frequently met upon Asiatic seals. The Scarabæus was esteemed as having thirty joints.

Mediæval thought, in accepting the idea of the Christian Trinity, lavishly threw its symbolism everywhere ; writers and symbolists, architects and heralds, multiplied ideas of three-fold qualities.

Heraldry is permeated with three-fold repetitions, a proportion of at least one-third of the generality of heraldic coats having a trinity of one sort or another. In all probability the stars and bars of America rose from the coat-armour of an English family in which the stars were three, the bars three.

St. Nicholas had as his attributes three purses, three bulls of gold, three children.

Sacred marks were three dots, sometimes alone, some-times in a triangle, sometimes in a double triangle ; three balls attached, making a trefoil ; three bones in a triangle crossing at the corners ; a fleur-de-lys in various designs of three conjoined ; three lines crossed by three lines ; and many other forms.

God, the symbolists said, was symbolized by a hexagon, whose sides were Glory, Power, Majesty, Wisdom, Blessing, and Honor. The three steps to heaven were Oratio, Amor, Imitatio. The three steps to the altar, the three spires of the cathedral, the three lancets of an Early English window, were all supposed to refer to the Trinity.

Having seen that the idea of the Trinity is a part of most of the ancient religious systems, it remains to point to one or two instances where, in common with other ideas from that source, the Trinity has a place among church grotesques.

There is a triune head in St. Mary's Church, Faversham, Kent, which was doubtless executed as indicative of the Trinity. The *Beehive of the Romishe Church*, in 1579, says: "They in their churches and Masse Bookes doe paint the Trinitie with three faces; for our mother the holie Church did learn that at Rome, where they were wont to paint or carve Janus with two faces." In the Salisbury Missal of 1534 is a woodcut of the Trinity triangle surmounted by a

A TRINITY, ST. MARY'S, FAVERSHAM.

three-faced head similar to the above. Hone reproduces it in his *Ancient Mysteries Described*, and asks, "May not the triune head have been originally suggested by the three-headed Saxon deity named "Trigla?" The Faversham tria, it will be noticed, has the curled and formal beards of the Greek mask.

Another instance of a three-fold head similar to the Faversham carving is at Cartmel.

A still more remarkable form of the same thing occurs as a rosette on the tomb of Bishop de la Wich, in Chichester Cathedral, in which the trinity of faces is doubled and placed in a circle in an exceedingly ingenious and symmetrical manner.   This has oak leaves issuing from the mouths, which we have seen as a frequent adjunct of the classic mask as indicating Jupiter.

DOUBLE TRINITY OF FOLIATE MASKS, CHICHESTER.

In carvings three will often be found to be a favourite number without a direct reference to the Trinity.   The form of the misericorde is almost invariably a three-part design, and, being purely arbitrary, its universal adoption is one of the evidences of the organization of the craft gild.

As with the misericorde, so with its subjects.   At Exeter we have seen (page 4) the tail of the harpy made into a trefoil ornament, while she grasps a trefoil-headed rod (just as among

Assyrian carvings we should have met a figure bearing the sacred three-headed poppy). At Gayton (page 87) we have the three-toothed flesh-hook; at Maidstone is another. Chichester Cathedral and Chichester Hospital have each three groups. Beverley Minster has three fish interlaced, and three

TRINITY OF MOWERS, WORCESTER.

hares running round inside a circle. In Worcester Cathedral there are three misericordes, in each of which there are three figures, in which groups the number is evidently intentional. Three till the ground, three reap corn with sickles, three mow with scythes.

From them as being unusual in treatment, even in this stiff Flemish set, is selected the trinity of mowers. Groups of three in mowing scenes is a frequent number. Doubtless this carving is indicative of July, that being the " Hey-Monath " of early times. One of the side supporters or pendant carvings of this is a hare riding upon the back of a leoparded lion, perhaps some reference to Leo, the sign governing July.

The three mowers do not make a pleasing carving, owing to the repetition and want of curve.

Other instances of triplication in Gothic design might be given, particularly in the choice of floral forms in which nature has set the pattern. This section, however, is chiefly important as a convenient means of incorporating a record of something further of the fundamental beliefs of the world's youth, connected with and extending the question of the remote origin of the ideas at the root of so many grotesques in church art.

The Fox in Church Art.

HE Fox, apostrophized as follows :

"O gentle one among the beasts of prey
O eloquent and comely-faced animal !"

as an important subject in mediæval art, has two distinct places.

There is a general impression that there was a great popular literary composition, running through many editions and through many centuries, having its own direct artistic illustration, and a wide indirect illustration which, later, by its ability to stand alone, had broken away from close connection with the epic, yet possessed a derivative identity with it.

Closer examination, however, proves that there is indeed the Fox in its particular literature with its avowed illustrations, but also that there is the Fox in mediæval art, illustrative of ideas partly found in literature, but illustrative of no particular work, and yet awaiting a key. Each is a separate and distinct thing.

Among the grotesques of our churches there are some references to the literary " Reynard the Fox," but they are few and far between ; while numerous most likely and prominent incidents of Reynard's career, as narrated in the poem, have no place among the carvings.

The subjects of the carvings are mostly so many variations of the idea of the Fox turned ecclesiastic and preying upon his care and congregation; and in this he is assisted by the ape, who also takes sides with him in carvings of other proceedings; but in none of these scenes is there evidence of reference to the epic. A great point of difference, too, lies in the conclusion of the epic, and the conclusion of Reynard's life as shewn in the carvings. In the epic, the King makes Reynard the Lord Chancellor and favourite.

The end of the Fox of church art, however, is far different; several sculptures agree in shewing him hanged by a body of geese.

In the epic, Reynard's victims are many. The deaths of the Hare and the Ram afford good circumstantial pictures, yet in the carvings there is neither of these; and it is scarcely Reynard who plots, and sins, and conceals, but a more vulgar fox who concerns himself, chiefly about geese, in an open, verminous way, while many of the sculptures are little more than natural history illustrations, in which we see *vulpes*, but not the Fox.

To enable, however, a fair comparison to be made between literature and art in this byway, it will be as well to glance at the history of the poem, and lay down a brief analysis of its episodes; and, next, to present sketches of some typical examples from the carvings.

Much of ancient satire owes its origin to that description

24

of fable which bestows the attributes and capacities of the human race upon the lower animals, which are made to reason and to speak. Their mental processes and their actions are entirely human, although their respective animal characteristics are often used to accentuate their human character. In every animal Edward Carpenter sees varying sparks of the actual mental life we call human, in, it may be added, arrested or perverted development, in which, in each instance, one characteristic has immeasurably prevailed. For the animal qualities, whether human or not in kind, man has ever had a sympathetic recognition, which has made both symbol and fable easily acceptable. Perhaps symbolism, which for so many ages has taken the various animals as figures to intelligibly express abstract qualities, gave rise to fable. If so, fable may be considered the grotesque of symbolism. The same ideas—of certain qualities—are taken from their original serious import, and used to amuse, and, while amusing, to strike.

On the other hand, Grimm asserts that animal-fable arose in the Netherlands, North France, and West Germany, extending neither to the Romance countries, nor to the Keltic; whereas we find animal symbolism everywhere. Grimm's statement may be taken to speak, perhaps, of a certain class of fable, and the countries he names are certainly where we should expect to find the free-est handling of superstitions. His arguments are based on the Germanic form of the names given to the beasts, but his localities seem to follow the course of the editions. Perhaps special causes, and not the influence of race, decided the localities. The earliest trace of a connected animal-fable is of that which is also the most wide-spread and popular—the history of the Fox.

This early production is a poem, called *Isengrinus*, in Latin hexameters, by a cleric of South Flanders, whose name has not survived.   It was written in the first half of the twelfth century, and first printed, it is said, so late as 1834.

In this, the narrative is briefly as follows :—The Lion is sick, and calls a court to choose his successor.   Reynard is the only animal that does not appear.   The Wolf, Isengrinus, to ruin Reynard's adherents, the Goat and the Ram, prescribes as a remedy for the Lion's disorder a medicine of Goat and Ram livers.   They defend the absent Reynard, and pronounce him a great doctor, and, to save their livers, drive the Wolf by force from before the throne.   Reynard is summoned. He comes with herbs, which, he says, will only be efficacious if the patient is wrapped in the skin of a wolf four years old. The Wolf is skinned, the Lion is cured, and Fox made Chancellor.

In this story is neatly dovetailed another, narrating how the Wolf had been prevented from devouring a party of weak pilgrim animals by the judicious display of a wolf's head. This head was cut off a wolf found hanging in a tree, and, at Reynard's instigation, the party, on the strength of possessing it, led the Wolf to believe them to be a company of professional wolf-slayers.

After this poem followed another at the end of the same

century with numerous additions and alterations, by a monk of Ghent. Next came a high German poem, also of the twelfth century, expanded, but without great addition. After this came the French version, Roman de Renart, which, with supplementary compositions, enlarged the matter to no less than 41,748 verses. There is another French version, called Renart le Contrefet, of nearly the same horrible length.

A Flemish version, written in the middle of the thirteenth century, and continued in the fourteenth, became the great father of editions.

All these were in verse, but on the invention of printing the Flemish form was re-cast into prose, and printed at Gouda in 1479, and at Delft in 1485; abridged and mutilated it was often re-printed in Holland.

Caxton printed a translation in 1481, and another a few years later. The English quarto, like the Dutch, also gave rise in time to a call for a cheap abridgment, and it appeared in 1639, as "The Most delectable history of Reynard the Fox."

Meanwhile a Low Saxon form had appeared, " Reinche Bos," first printed at Lubeck in 1498, and next at Rostock in 1517, a translation, with alterations, from the Flemish publication. Various other editions in German followed, with cuts by Amman.

In all these and their successors the incidents were varied. Having seen that, within at least certain limits, the story must have been exceedingly well-known and popular, we will run through the incidents narrated in the most popular of the

German Reynard poems, chiefly taken from Goethe's rendering.

Nouvel, the Lion, calls a parliament, and the Fox does not appear, and is accused of various crimes. The Wolf accuses him of sullying the honour of his wife, and blinding his three children. A little Dog accuses him of stealing a pudding end (this the Cat denies, stating that the pudding was one of her own stealing). The Leopard accuses him of murder, having only the day before rescued the Hare from his clutch as he was throttling him, under pretence of severity in teaching the Creed.

The Badger, Grimbart, now comes forward in defence.

> " An ancient proverb says, quoth he,
> Justice in an enemy
> Is seldom to be found."

He accuses the Wolf in his turn of violating the bonds of partnership. The Fox and the Wolf had arranged to rob a fish-cart. The Fox lay for dead on the road, and the carter, taking him up, threw him on the top of the load of fish, turning to his horse again. Reynard then threw the fish on to the road, and jumping down to join in the feast found left for him but fin and scales. The Badger explains away also the story of Reynard's guilt as to Dame Isengrin, and, with regard to the Hare, asks if a teacher shall not chastise his scholars. In short, since the King proclaimed a peace, Reynard was thoroughly reformed, and but for being absorbed in penance would no doubt have been present to defend himself from any false reports.

Unfortunately for this justification, at the very moment of its conclusion a funeral procession passes ;

> " On sable bier
> The relics of a Hen appear,"

while Henning, the Cock, makes a piteous complaint of Reynard's misdeeds.   He said how the Fox had

> " Assured him he'd become a friar,
> And brought a letter from his prior ;
> Show'd him his hood and shirt of hair,
> His rosary and scapulaire ;
> Took leave of him with pious grace,
> That he might hasten to his place
> To read the nona and the sept,
> And vesper too before he slept ;
> And as he slowly took his way,
> Read in his pocket breviary."

all of which ended in the devout penitent eating nineteen of Henning's brood.

The Lion invites his council's advice.   It is decided to send an envoy to Reynard, and Bruno, the Bear, is selected to summon him to court.

Bruno finds him at his castle of Malepart, and thunders a summons.   Reynard, by plausible speech and a story of honey, disarms some of his hostility, and entices him off to a carpenter's yard, where an oak trunk, half split, yet has the wedge in.   Reynard declaring the honey is in the cleft, Bruno puts his head and paws in.   Reynard draws out the wedge. The Bear howls till the whole village is aroused, and Bruno, to save his life, draws himself out minus skin from head and paws. In the confusion the parson's cook falls into the stream, and the parson offers two butts of beer to the man who saves her. While this is being done, the Bear escapes, and the Fox taunts him.

The Bear displaying his condition at court, the King swears to hang Reynard, this time sending Hinge, the Cat, to summon Reynard to trial. Hinge is lured to the parson's house in hopes of mice, and caught in a noose fixed for Reynard. The household wake, and beat the Cat, who dashes underneath the priest's robe, revenging himself in a cruel and unseemly way. The Cat is finally left apparently dead, but reviving, gnaws the cord, and crawls back to court.

"The King was wroth, as wroth could be."

The Badger now offers to go, three times being the necessary number for summoning a peer of the realm. He puts the case plainly before Reynard, who agrees to come, and they set out together. On the way Reynard has a fit of remorse, and confesses his sins. Grimbart plucks a twig, makes the Fox beat himself, leap over it three times, kiss it; and then declares him free from his sins. All the time Reynard casts a greedy eye on some chickens, and makes a dash at one shortly after. Accused by Grimbart, he declares he had only looked aside to murmur a prayer for those who die in "yonder cloister."

> "And also I would say
> A prayer for the endless peace
> Of many long-departed geese,
> Which, when in a state of sin,
> I stole from the nuns who dwell therein,"

The Fox arrives at court with a proud step and a bold eye. He is accused, but

> " Tried every shift and vain pretence
> To baffle truth and common sense,
> And shield his crimes with eloquence."

In vain. He is condemned to die. His friend Martin the Ape, Grimbart the Badger, and others withdraw in resentment, and the King is troubled.

At the gallows Reynard professes to deliver a dying confession, and introduces a story of seven waggon-loads of gold and jewels which had been a secret hoard of his father, stolen for the purpose of bribing chiefs to depose the Lion and place the Bear on the throne.

Reynard is pardoned on condition of pointing out the treasure. He declares it to be in Husterlo, but excuses himself from accompanying the King on his way there, as he, Reynard, is excommunicated for once assisting the Wolf to escape from a monastery, and must, therefore, go to Rome to get absolution.

The King announces his pardon to the court. The Bear and Wolf are thrown into prison, and Reynard has a scrip made of a piece of the Bear's hide, and shoes of the skin of the feet of the Wolf and his wife. Blessed by Bellin the Ram, who is the King's chaplain, and accompanied a short distance by the whole court, he sets out for Rome. The chaplain Ram and Lampe the Hare, accompany him home to bid his wife farewell. He inveigles the Hare inside, and the family eat him. He puts the Hare's head in the bear-skin

wallet, and taking it to the impatient Bellin outside, asks him
to take it to the King, as it contains letters of state policy.

The satchel is opened in full court, and Reynard once
more proclaimed a traitor, accursed and banned, the Bear and
Wolf restored, and the Ram and all his race given to them for
atonement.   A twelve-day tourney is held.   On the eighth
day the Coney and the Crow present complaint against
Reynard ; he had wounded the Coney, and eaten the Crow's
wife.   It is resolved, in spite of the Lioness's second inter-
cession, to besiege Malepart and hang Reynard.

Grimbart secretly runs off to warn Reynard, who decides
to return to court once more and plead his cause.   They set
out together, and Reynard again confesses his sins.   This
introduces a story of how he once fooled the Wolf.   Isengrin
coveted to eat a foal, and sent the Fox to inquire the price
from the mare.   She replied the price was written on her
hinder hoof.   The Fox, seeing the trick, returned to the
Wolf saying he could not understand the inscription.   The
Wolf boasts of his learning, having long ago taken his
degrees as Doctor of Both Faculties.   The Wolf bends down
to examine the newly-shod hoof, and the rest may be supposed.

On their way to court, Reynard and Grimbart meet
Martin the Ape, who is bound for Rome, and promises his
gold shall buy Reynard's absolution.   Arrived at court,
Reynard boldly explains away the stories of the Coney and
the Crow, and demands the trial by battle.   The Coney and
Crow, having no witnesses, and being averse to battle,
withdraw.   Reynard accuses the dead Bellin of killing the

Hare Lampe and secreting rare jewels he sent to the King. His story is half believed in the hope that the jewels, which he described at great length, may be found. Reynard's former services to the state are remembered, and he is about to depart triumphant, when the Wolf, unable to restrain his rage, accuses him afresh. In the end, as each accusation is smoothly foiled, he accepts the wager of battle. They withdraw to prepare for the lists. Reynard is shorn and shaven, all but his tail, by his relatives the Apes. He is well oiled. He is also enjoined to drink plentifully overnight.

They meet in the lists. Reynard kicks up the dust to blind the Wolf, draws his wet tail across his eyes, and at length tears an eye out. He is, however, seized by the Wolf's strong jaw, and is about to be finished off when he takes advantage of a word of parley to seize the wolf in a tender part with his hand, and the fight recommences, ending in the total overthrow of Isengrin. The King orders the fray to be stayed and the Wolf's life spared. The Wolf is carried off. All fly to congratulate the victor,

> " All gazed in his face with fawning eyes,
>   And loaded him with flatteries."

The King makes him the Lord Chancellor and takes him to his close esteem.

The tale winds up :

> " To wisdom now let each one turn,
>   Avoid the base and virtue learn ;
>   This is the end of Reynard's story,
>   May God assist us to His glory."

The above is the gist of the matter dealing with the
Fox in letters ; from these lively images we will turn to the
more wooden achievements of the carvers.   The general
fact that the Fox is a marauder specially fond of the flesh of
that bird of long descent, the goose, but also partial to that of
other birds, is frequently illustrated by church carvings.   In
the churches at the following places he is carved as having
seized his prey :— Beverley (Minster), Boston, Fairford,

THE FOX RETURNING FROM HUNTING, MANCHESTER.

Faversham, Gloucester, Hereford, Norwich, Oxford (Mag-
dalen), Peterborough, Ripon, Wellingborough, Winchester,
and Windsor (St. George's Chapel).   At the last-named
he is also shewn as preying upon a hen.   At Beverley (Minster),
Ely, Manchester, and Thanet (St. Mary's Minster) the picture
of the abduction of the goose is heightened in interest by his
pursuit by a woman armed with a distaff.   Doubtless there

are others ; the object throughout is to give examples, not an exhaustive list.

A somewhat unusual subject is one in Manchester Cathedral, in which the Fox is returning from hunting. A carving where the Fox is used to point a moral is another, in St. George's Chapel, Windsor, in which three monks, conveyed in a wheel-barrow into Hell's Mouth, are accompanied by a Fox with a goose in his mouth. Probably the idea here broadly expressed is intended to be quietly suggested by some of the above.

Next in frequency is the more definite satire of the Fox preaching to Geese. We find it at Beverley (both the Minster and St. Mary's), Boston, Bristol, Cartmel, Ely, Etchingham, Nantwich, Ripon, Stowlangtoft, and Windsor (St. George's Chapel). In the last he has a goose in his cowl.

All those need for their completion the supposition that the text of the Fox's sermon is the same as was given at length in a representation of a preaching scene on an ancient stained-glass window in the church of St. Martin, Leicester, which was unhappily destroyed in the last century. In this, from the Fox's mouth proceeded the words "Testis est mihi Deus, quam cupiam vos omnes visceribus meus" (God is my witness how I desire you all in my bowels.—Philippians, i., 8). In Wolfius, A.D. 1300, is a description of another such representation, in a MS. of Æsop's Fables. It may accord quite well with the theory of the transmission of designs by the continuity of the artificers' gild system to suppose that some proportion of the material found its way into their repertoire through the medium of manuscripts (not necessarily original in them), especially for such subjects as were essentially mediæval. We have seen how the carvings of Jonah and of Samson, at Ripon, were taken from the Poor Man's Bible ; here we have the Preaching Fox mentioned in a book of 1300 as being in an earlier work. A Fox bearing two Cocks by the neck on a staff is the initial T in a MS. considered by Montfaucon to be of the ninth century. Fredegarius, the Frankish historian, in the middle of the seventh century, has a fable of a Fox at the court of the Lion, repeated by others in the tenth and eleventh. Paulin Paris and Thomas Wright agreed in thinking the whole fable of French origin, and first in the Latin tongue. So that we may reasonably suppose that the countless tons of books and MSS. (though it is useless to grope now among the mere memories of ashes), burnt at the Reformation, would contain much that would have made clearer our understanding of this subject of Gothic grotesques. It is clear, however, that the Fox was used as a means of satirical comment before the writing of the Isengrine Fable, and that most of the church carvings refer to what we may call pre-Fable or co-Fable conceptions.

There may be other material lying hidden in our great libraries, but search for early Reynard drawings produces almost nothing.

At Ripon the Fox is shewn without vestments, in a neat Gothic pulpit adorned with carvings of the trefoil.* His

* The Church Treasury, by William Andrews, 1898, p. 193.

hands, and what they may have held, are gone. His congregation is to his right a goose, to his left a cock, who appear
to be uttering responses, while his face is significant of
conscious slyness.

In Beverley Minster the Preaching Fox is in a square
panelled pulpit on four legs ; before him are seven geese, one
of whom slumbers peacefully.   He wears a gown and cowl,
has a rosary in his right hand, and appears to be performing
his part with some animation.   Behind the pulpit stands an
ape with a goose hung on a stick, while another fox—to give
point to the lesson—is slinking off with a goose slung over his

THE PREACHING FOX, RIPON.

back.   At St. Mary's, Beverley, the various carvings have a
decidedly manuscript appearance.   The one of the Preaching
Fox has labels, upon which, in some unknown original, may
have been inscribed texts or other matter.   Here the Fox
wears only his " scapulaire," and has his right hand raised in
correct exhortative manner ; his pulpit is of stone, and is
early.   Behind stand two persons, perhaps male and female,
whose religious dress would lead us to suppose them to
represent the class to whose teaching a fox-like character is to
be attributed.   At the front are seated two apes, also in

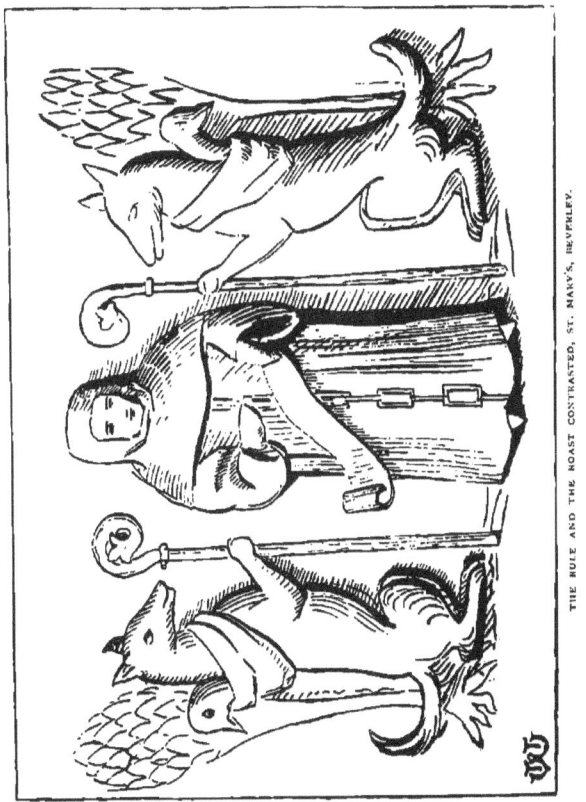

THE RULE AND THE ROAST CONTRASTED, ST. MARY'S, BEVERLEY.

scapularies, or hoods, who, as well as the Fox, may be here
to shew the real character of the supposed sanctified.

It will have been noticed how frequently the carvings
evade explanation ; all these satires on the clergy may mean
either that the system was bad, or that there was much abuse
of it. A remarkable instance of this is in another misericorde
in St. Mary's, Beverley. Here we have the Benedictine with
mild and serene countenance, without a sign of sin, and bearing

THE PREACHING FOX, ST. MARY'S, BEVERLEY.

the scroll of truth and simplicity of life—call it the rule of his
order. Yet how do many of his followers act? With greed
for the temporalities, they aspire to the pastoral crook, and
devour their flocks with such rapacity as to threaten the
up-rooting of the whole order.

Such might be one rendering ; yet the placid cleric may
be simply introduced to shew the outward appearance of the
ravening ones.

26

It has been a favourite explanation of these anti-cleric carvings to say that they were due to the jealousy which existed between the regular orders and the preaching friars. But carvings such as this last are sufficient to prove the explanation erroneous ; preaching friars carried no croziers.

Yet another instance from St. Mary's shews us two foxes in scapularies reading from a book placed on an eagle-lectern.

The bird—lectern or not—has round its head a kind of

FOXES AT THE LECTERN, ST. MARY'S, BEVERLEY.

aureola or glory ; it is probably an eagle, but who shall say it is not a dove ? The religiously-garbed foxes are alone unmistakable.

At Boston we have a mitred Fox, enthroned in the episcopal seat in full canonicals, clutching at a cock which stands near, while another bird is at the side. Close by the throne, another fox, in a cowl only, is reading from a book.

At Christchurch, Hampshire, we see the Fox on a seat-elbow, in a pulpit of good design, and near him, on a stool, the Cock; it appears in the initial of this article.

At Worcester, a scapularied Fox is kneeling before a small table or altar, laying his hand with an affectation of reverence upon—a sheep's head. This is one of the side carvings to the misericorde of the three mowers, considered under the head of "Trinities."

The Fox seizing the Hen, at Windsor, reminds of the

EPISCOPAL HYPOCRISY, BOSTON.

Fable, yet in so many other instances it is the Cock who is the prey. Still further removing the carvings out of the sphere of the Fable is a carving at Chicester of the Fox playing the harp to a goose, while an ape dances; and another at St. George's, Windsor, in which it is an ape who wears the stole, and is engaged in the laying on of hands. In the Fable the Fox teaches the Hare the Creed, yet in a carving at Manchester it is his two young cubs whom he is teaching from a book.

The Fox in the Shell of Salvation, artfully discoursing on the merits of a bottle of holy water, as drawn on page 58, may be considered a Preaching Fox.

There is at Nantwich a carving which, unlike any of those already noticed, is closely illustrative of an incident of the epic. It represents the story told to Nouvel's court by the widower Crow. He and his wife, in travelling through the country, came across what they thought was the dead body of Reynard on the heath. He was stiff, his tongue protruded, his eyes were inverted. They lamented his unhappy fate, and "course so early run." The lady approached his chin, not, indeed, with any idea of commencing a meal ; far from that, it was to ascertain if perchance any signs of life remained, when—snap! Her head was off! The Crow himself had the melancholy luck to fly to a tree, there to sit and watch his wife eaten up. In the carving we have the crows first coming upon the sight of the counterfeit carrion as it lies near a rabbit warren. To shew how perfect is Reynard's semblance of death, the rear portions of two rabbits are to be seen as they hurry into their holes on the approach of the crows, the proximity of the Fox not having previously alarmed them.

The side figures have no simultaneous connection with the central composition, being merely representations of Reynard, once more as a larder regarder. The pilgrim's hat, borne by one of the figures, is a further reminder of the Fable, and the monkish garb is of course in keeping. These

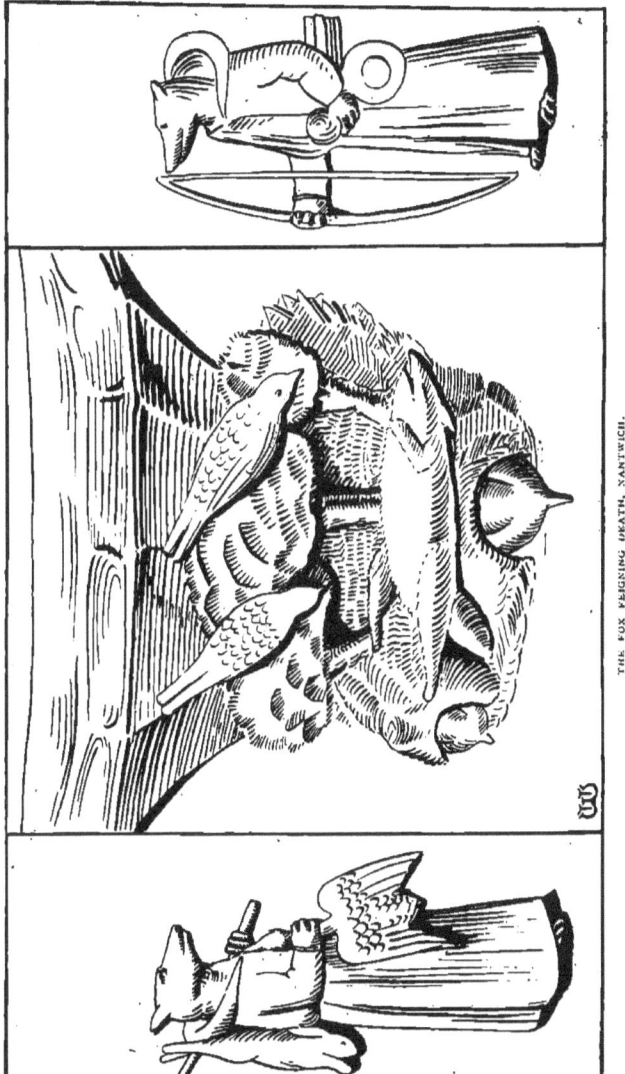

THE FOX FEIGNING DEATH, NANTWICH.

two are somewhat singular in being fox-headed men. At Chester, also, is a Fox feigning death.

Thus far the examples have been of Reynard's crimes; we will now survey his punishment. In the fable he was to be hanged, but was not, the Wolf and the Bear, whom he always outwitted, being the disappointed executioners. In the carvings he is really hanged, and the hangsmen are the geese

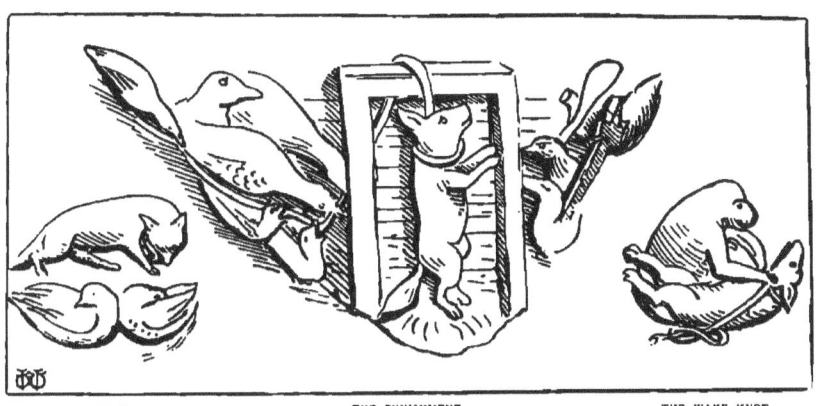

THE TEMPTATION.   THE PUNISHMENT.   THE WAKE KNOT.
BEVERLEY MINSTER.

of his despoliation. Beverley Minster has among its fine carvings an admirable rendering of this subject. Reynard is hanged on a square gallows, a number of birds, geese, taking a beak at the rope. To the left of the gallows stand two official geese, with mace and battle-axe. The left supplementary carving gives a note of the crime; Reynard is creeping upon two sleeping geese. The right hand supporting carving gives us the Fox after being cut down. His friend, the Ape,

is untying the rope from his neck.   Observe the twist of the
rope at the end; it declares that Reynard is dead, for it is a
Wake Knot!

Also at Boston, Bristol, Nantwich, and Sherborne are
carvings of the hanging by geese.   The gallows of the Sherborne execution is square, and made of rough trees.   The
general action is less logical than in the Beverley scene, but
the geese are full of vivacity, evidently enjoying the thorough-

EXECUTION OF REYNARD, SHERBORNE.

ness with which they are carrying out their intentions.

In the hanging scenes there is no suggestion of the
religious dress.   Reynard has lost his Benefit of Clergy.
Besides the carving of the Ape laying out the dead Fox, at
Beverley there are also others where the Ape is riding on the
Fox's back, and again where he is tending him in bed.   The
Ape succouring the Fox is also instanced at Windsor.

However, after the two broad classes of carvings are exhausted—the Fox deluding or eating birds, and the Fox hanged by birds, there is little left to tell of him.

It may be added that his hanging by his one-time victims has suggested to the carver another subject of the same kind—the hanging of the cat by mice, or, more probably, rats, mentioned on page 43. It is there stated to be at Sherborne, in error, the place being Great Malvern.

EXECUTION OF THE CAT, GREAT MALVERN.

The following curious scene from the Fox-fruitful church of St. Mary's, Beverley, is perplexing, and gives the Fox receiving his quietus under unique circumstances. He is, with anxiety, awaiting the diagnosis of an ape-doctor, who is critically examining urinary deposits ; his health has been evidently not all he could wish. When, lo, an arrow, from the bow of an archer in quilted leather, pierces him through the heart ! What more this carving means is a mystery.

27

Carvings of the ordinary fables in which the Fox is concerned are not unknown. At Faversham, Kent, is one of the Fox and the Grapes; at Chester is the Fox and the Stork. The latter is, again, on a remarkable slab, probably a coffin lid, in the Priory Church of Bridlington, East Yorkshire, the strange combination of designs on which may be described. At the head appear two curious dragon forms

REYNARD IN DANGER, ST. MARY'S, BEVERLEY.

opposed over an elaborate embattled temple, suggestive of Saxon and Byzantine derivation, with a central pointed arch. This may be a rendering of the sun-myth, noted on page 37. At the foot is a reversed lion, the curls and twists of whose mane and tail closely resembles those of the white porcelain lions used by the Chinese as incense-burners. Between the temple and the lion is incised an illustration of the fable of the Fox and the Stork. The slab, of which a rough sketch is annexed, is of black basaltic marble, similar to that of the font of the church, which is of the type generally considered to be Norman, and to have been imported ready made from Flanders, and on which dragons are sometimes the ornament. The Fox on this slab is the earliest sculptured figure of the animal known in England.

There are also hunting scenes in which the fox is shot with bow and arrow, as in Beverley Minster ; or chased with hounds in a way more commending itself to modern sporting ideas, as at Ripon.

In conclusion, the satirical intent of the fox inventions, as we find them in the library or in the church, may be summed up, for here indeed lies the whole secret of their prevalence and popularity. The section of society satirized by the epic is large, but is principally covered by the feudal institution. The notes struck are its greed of wealth and its greed of the table, its injustice under the pretext of

COFFIN LID, BRIDLINGTON, YORKSHIRE.

laws, its expedient lying, the immunity from punishment afforded by riches, the absolute yet revolution-fearing power of the sovereign, the helplessness of nobles single-handed, and the general influence of religion thrown over everything, while for its own sake being allowed to really influence nothing.

The chief point of the epic is generally considered to be that power in the hands of the feudal barons was accompanied by a trivial amount of intelligence, which was easily deceived by the more astute element of society. The carvings give no note of this. A further object, however, may be seen. The whole story of the Fox is meant not only to shew that

> " It is not strength that always wins,
> For wit doth strength excel,"

by playing on the passions and weaknesses of mankind, but in particular to hold up to scorn the immunity procured by professional religion, though it is fair to note that the Fox does not adopt a religious life because suited to his treacherous and deceitful character, but to conceal it. Thus so far as they elucidate the general "foxiness" of religious hypocrisy, the carvings and the epic illustrate the same theme, but it is evident that they embodied and developed already-existing popular recognition of the evil, each in its own way, and without special reference one to the other.

Situations of the Grotesque Ornament in Church Art.

THE places chosen for the execution of the work which, by reason of its intention or its want of conformity with what we now consider a true taste in art, may be styled Grotesque, do not seem to be in any marked degree different from the situations selected for other ornamental work. It may, however, be permitted to glance at those situations, and enquire as to such comparisons as they afford, though the conclusions to be arrived at must necessarily be loose and general.

In Norman work the chief iconographical interest is to be found in the capitals of pilasters and pillars, for here is often told a story of some completeness. Other places are the arches, chiefly of doorways ; bosses of groining, and the horizontal corners of pillar plinths ; exteriorly, the gargoyles are most full of meaning, seconded by the corbels of the corbel-table. We may expect in Norman grotesque some reference to ancient mystics ; the forms are bold and rugged, such appearance of delicacy as exists being attained by inter-lacing lines in conventional patterns, with, also, the effect of distance upon repeating ornament.

Transitional Norman retained all the characteristic or-nament of the purer style, but with the development of Early

English the grotesque for a time somewhat passed out of vogue, slight but eminently graceful modifications of the Corinthian acanthus supplying most of the places where strange beasts had formerly presented their bewildering shapes. It might not be impossible to connect this partial purification of ornament with a phase of church history.

But in some portions of structure, as the gargoyles, and in the woodwork of the choirs, the grotesque still held its

APE CORBEL, CARRYING ROOF
TIMBER, KWELME.

own. As Early English grew distinctly into the Decorated, every available spot was enriched with carving. The collections (called "portfolios" elsewhere) of the old carvers would seem to have been ransacked and exhausted, all that had gone before receiving fresh rendering in wood and stone, while life and nature were now often called upon to furnish new material. The pointed arch remained, however, an undecorated sweep of mouldings, and the plinth corners were rarely touched; in fact there was here scarcely now the same squareness of space which before had asked for ornament. All the other places ornamented in Norman work were filled up in Decorated with the new designs of old subjects. The resting-places of ornament were multiplied; the dripstones of every kind of arch, and the capitals of every kind of pillar, whether in the arcading of the walls, the heaped-up richness of the reredos, or the single

MISERICORDE—LION COMPOSITION, WELLINGBOROUGH.

subject of the piscina, became nests of the grotesque. In a single group of sedilia all the architecture of a great cathedral may be seen in miniature, in arch, column, groined roof, boss, window-tracery, pinnacle, and finial, each part with its share of ornament, of grotesque. In the choirs the carvers had busied themselves with summoning odd forms from out the hard oak, till the croches or elbow-rests, the bench ends, the stall canopies, and below all, and above all, the misericordes, swarmed with all the ideas of Asia and Europe past and present. Musicians are everywhere, but most persistently on the intersections of the choir arches, and somewhat less so on those of the nave.

A favourite place for humourous figures was on the stone brackets or corbels which bear up timber roofs ; examples are in the ape corbel in this article, and the responsible yet happy-looking saint at the end of the list of Contents.

When the Perpendicular style came with other arts from Italy, and the lavish spread of the Decorated was chastened and over-chastened into regularity, there came for the second or third time the same ideas from the never-dying mythologies, their concrete embodiments sometimes with eloquence rendered, nearly always with vigour. They came to the old places, but in most fulness to that most full place, the dark recess where lurks the misericorde.

Upon the whole it would appear that the grotesque, be it in the relics of a long-forgotten symbolism, in crude attempts at realism, or in the fantastic whimseys of irresponsibility, is chiefly met in the portions of the church where would occur,

28

in the development of architecture, the problems and diffi-
culties.   They occur, so to speak, at the joints of construction.
It may be that the pluteresques (grotesque and other ornaments made of metal) employed in many Spanish churches
are to be accounted for in this way on the score of the facility
of attachment.   Where it may be questioned that the ornament was to conceal juncture, it is often to be acknowledged
that it was to give external apparent lightness to masses which
are in themselves joints or centres of weight.   To conclude
—to whatever extent we may carry our inquiries into the
meaning of the grotesques in church art, we have in them
undoubtedly objects whose associations are among the most
ancient of the human race; whatever our opinion of their
fitness for a place in the temple, it is plain that practically
they could be nowhere else.

MUSICIAN ON THE INTERSECTION OF NAVE ARCHES,
ST. HELEN'S, ABINGDON, BERKSHIRE.

⇒ INDEX. ⇐

Index.

INDEX.

INDEX.

www.ingramcontent.com/pod-product-compliance
Lightning Source LLC
Chambersburg PA
CBHW020114030726
47498CB00006B/2101